LAMENTATION

Also by Joe Clifford

The Jay Porter Novels
December Boys

Nonseries
Wake the Undertaker

Memoir
Junkie Love

Anthologies
Choice Cuts
Trouble in the Heartland (editor)

LAMENTATION
A NOVEL

JOE CLIFFORD

Longboat Key, Florida

ISBN: 978-1-60809-185-0

Published in the United States of America by Oceanview Publishing
Longboat Key, Florida

www.oceanviewpub.com
10 9 8 7 6 5 4 3 2

PRINTED IN THE UNITED STATES OF AMERICA

For my brothers, Josh and Jason

ACKNOWLEDGMENTS

I would like to thank my lovely wife, Justine, who gives me the time and space to create—and who later lends the critical eye to make my books better; and my son, Holden, for making me believe in the better parts of me.

Thanks to my agent, Elizabeth Kracht—a giant teddy bear can't begin to show my appreciation; and to Frank, Pat, Bob, Emily, David, and everyone on the Oceanview team for taking a chance on me.

Thanks to the crime and mystery writing community. It never fails to amaze that the folks who write about murder, mayhem, and worse are, to a person, some of the kindest and most generous people I've ever met.

And, finally, thanks to my family, fans, and readers of my work. Your support is why I do this.

LAMENTATION

CHAPTER ONE

I had ducked inside the pantry to see what else we could sell when I tripped over a cord of wood and snared the back of my work coat on an old, rusty nail. The sharp point tore through the thick padding and ripped a hole in my long johns, all the way through my undershirt. I hurried to the sink and peeled off the layers. Just a surface cut. Thankfully, unlike the heat and power, the water was still on. I dabbed at the wound. Last thing I needed was lockjaw. I hadn't had a tetanus shot in twelve years. The estate clearing business was big in Ashton, and my boss, Tom Gable, a good guy, but it's not like the gig came with health insurance.

All afternoon I'd been up at Ben Saunders' place, a two-hundred-year-old farmhouse in the foothills, cherry picking through the dead man's belongings, loading the U-Haul for trips to flea markets and swap shops in southern New England. Saunders had lived alone and was a packrat. The cancer finally got him around Thanksgiving. Most of his stuff was junk. A dumpster sat in the snow-covered driveway overflowing with waterlogged pads of fiberglass, chunks of splintered wood, jagged shards of glass, trash bags jam-packed with leftovers that didn't quite translate to dollars and cents. I was almost done, and I'd be glad for the day to end. If I wrapped up soon enough, I'd have time to shoot across town to catch Jenny before she put our son to bed. I hadn't seen him all week.

Out the kitchen window, thick, black storm clouds roiled over Lamentation Mountain, churning like the gears to a violent machine, steamrolling the summit and sucking all light from the landscape, pastures and stonewalls shrouded in dense fields of leaden smoke. Cold winds rustled through broken windows. The flapping insulation sounded like a plastic bag held out a speeding car on the highway.

The big, empty farmhouse smelled of abandon. Night was settling, and the snow began to fall heavier. It had been one of the worst winters on record. Certainly, the worst since the accident.

Twenty years had passed but my parents' crash felt closer to last week. I stared in the direction of Lamentation Bridge, even though I couldn't see much through the evening gloaming, freezing my ass off, making no effort to get redressed. I knew that somewhere in the dark lay the exact spot where their brakes had failed, and they plunged into the frigid gray water of Echo Lake; the night everything had changed for my older brother, Chris, and me. I could feel death's presence lurking the entire week I'd been working there, a pall hanging over the place. It was the monkey on my back. The elephant in the room. The crazy little bird chirping in my ear.

The headlights from Tom's truck fanned up the gravel drive, slicing through snowy pines and shining into my eyes.

I pulled my ripped shirt over my head and bundled back up, then headed outside to greet him.

Tom climbed down from the cab and lumbered over, broad shoulders curled, hands jammed in pockets. I could hear my untied work boots crunching frozen dirt and snow as harsh winds raced through the valley.

"Almost done," I shouted above the din of engine and storm, nodding back at the old farmhouse. "Maybe one and a half, two hours left."

Tom gestured for me to follow him back to his idling Ford F-350, which rumbled like a washing machine stuck with an uneven load. We hoisted ourselves into the warm cab, welcoming the hot air blasting through the vents.

I pulled the Marlboros from my coat and cupped my hands to light one. The radio softly hummed. The Allman Brothers, "Sweet Melissa." That song had been playing the first time I kissed Jenny in Steve Ryba's basement back in high school. Always hit me hard. Tom offered me the other half of a ham and cheese from the Gas 'n' Go, but I shook him off. Last time I'd made the mistake of eating a gas station sandwich, I spent half the night with my face stuck in the toilet.

Tom reached in his coat and passed along an envelope.

By its heft, I could tell that there had to be at least a grand in there.

Tom was a good boss and treated me well. But the nature of estate clearing meant nothing was permanent, and the brutal winters often made it difficult to transport merchandise. Which frequently spelled downtime for me—downtime I didn't want. A thousand bucks said we were looking at another one of those times.

"That should hold you over a few," he said.

"If it doesn't," I said, tucking the envelope into my coat, "that's not your problem."

"Yeah, it is. You're the best guy I got, Jay. I hate doing this to you, but everything slows down this time of year. You know that."

I nodded.

"Might have another place up in Berlin. But that won't be for at least three weeks. Finding somewhere to sell the shit, that's another matter." He forced a laugh. "Helluva place to run antiques." His frost-burned cheeks winced a grin through the bushy beard that covered two-thirds of his face.

I gazed out the window. Distant lights flickered on the range like fireflies in a jar in the summer, as families retreated safely inside to batten down hatches and weather the latest storm.

I made for the handle. "Still a few things inside I have to pack. I've got a pair of floodlights in my truck I can use. I want to wrap this up for you today."

"Don't worry about it," Tom said. "I'll take care of it."

I didn't like the way he looked when he said that. Because I knew what was coming next. I'd been getting that look since my mom and dad had died, ever since my brother had turned into what he'd become. It spelled a long night of aggravation.

"Turley's looking for you," he said.

He didn't need to add the next part, but he did anyway. "They got Chris down at the station."

CHAPTER TWO

Lamentation Mountain was a misnomer, since it wasn't actually one mountain but a whole range of them, divided by the main thoroughfare of the Desmond Turnpike, which ran south all the way to Concord and north across the border into Montreal. There were no roads out of town to the east, and the only route west traversed the treacherous Ragged Pass, an icy deathtrap most of the year.

The Ashton Police Station was deep in the flats, across Camel's Back and past Axel Rod Road. As I descended the ridge, snow dumped in big clumps, glopping on everything like wet, sticky rice, obscuring traffic lights and stop signs. The sporadic streetlamps couldn't make a dent in the dark, which made the short ride take a lot longer than it should have. Not that I was in any rush to get there.

I'd lost count of how many times I'd picked up my asshole brother over the years. Shoplifting at the Price Chopper. Dealing at the TC Truck Stop. Garden-variety vagrancy. We were a small town, and people rarely pressed charges, but, still, it was embarrassing. Usually, they'd stick my big brother in a tiny cell for a night or two, then release him to me. Who else were they going to call? Chris was Ashton's village idiot. And he was my problem.

The police station was brand-spanking new, part of the recently remodeled Town Centre. A few years ago, Ashton placed a measure on the ballot to allocate more police funds. Lombardi Construction got behind it, so it passed without a fight. Why wouldn't Lombardi support the measure? They'd be building the damned thing. With Michael Lombardi in the state senate and Adam Lombardi running the construction business, the family was the closest thing to royalty we had. Their dad, Gerry, even coached the high school wrestling team, on which Chris used to star back in the day, and the old man served on the board of UpStart, a mentoring program for at-risk boys throughout northern New Hampshire. Whenever he'd had too much to drink, Chris invariably would evoke the slight of having been left off the All-State team as the reason for his downfall. My brother never ran out of injustices to blame.

Besides the precinct, the renovated Centre also included a senior living facility, the library, and town hall. In a town of under three thousand, adding extra squad cars and a new holding cell smacked of overkill. But the drug epidemic up here was getting out of hand. At least that had been the posturing by local media. A recent poll in the *Herald* claimed that over half of high school students had admitted to trying some narcotic before tenth grade, if nothing more than popping the occasional painkiller from mom's stash. According to the paper, drug use had become "a blight and a scourge on the community." That may've been hyperbole, but it didn't take much to put the fear of God into God-fearing people.

Not that there wasn't a drug problem, especially at the truck stop, which was where most of those people seemed to congregate, setting up shop next door at the Maple Motor Inn, or in one of the sleazy motels along the Desmond Turnpike, waiting for their welfare checks on the first and fifteenth of every month. I'd seen firsthand the drug problem in Ashton, but giving cops shiny new toys to play with wasn't going to change anything; people were going to do whatever the hell they wanted to do.

***

When I stepped into the police station lobby, the bright fluorescents stabbed the backs of my eyeballs, and the jacked-up heat gave me an instant headache. Remnants from the holidays adorned the office—homemade Frosty the Snowman cards from Willard Elementary, half a sleigh bell streamer hanging from an eave—even though Christmas had been over a month ago. The septic smells of warmed microwaved foods overpowered the small space and only made my head hurt worse.

I clomped my boots on the mat by the door, drawing the attention of Claire Sizemore, who'd graduated with my brother, ten years ahead of me. She was the only one in the office, sitting at a desk in a neat row of three by the window, doing a sudoku puzzle or something. She gave me a sheepish wave and hefted herself to her feet. Her dull, brown hair frizzed in a do-it-yourself dye job, and her languid eyes drooped like maple syrup from a freshly tapped tree. Each time I saw Claire, I'd recall the time I caught my brother fingering her behind the fried dough booth at the Chesterton Bazaar.

The Chesterton Bazaar's a big deal when you're in the third grade and don't know any better, the rinky-dink rides and games only growing lamer each passing year. I was just a kid and didn't know exactly what Chris had been doing, but by the way Claire squealed it was clear she liked it. The clanking, old Ferris wheel chains chugged overhead and the hot oil of frying dough sizzled, as I watched him probe deeper and deeper. When he finally turned and saw me, my brother didn't look like he was having any fun.

"How are you, Jay?" Claire asked, leaning over the counter. "How's Aiden?"

"Getting big."

"Almost, what? Two?"

"In April."

"I ran into Jenny and Brody the other day at McDonald's. Aiden wasn't with them. Jenny said he was at her mom's?"

"Lynne babysits some mornings so Jenny can catch up on sleep after work."

"That Brody's an interesting character." Claire waited for my response.

I gave a halfhearted nod.

Claire's face sagged like an old hound dog. "I always liked you two together," she said, her voice tinged with sadness. "Jay and Jenny. Sounds cute, don't it?"

"Turley around?"

She motioned behind her. "Went for some coffee in the break room. Should be back in a minute. You here about your brother?" There was that look again.

I forced a grin, but probably couldn't hide my aggravation. I mean, why the hell else would I be there?

A moment later, Rob Turley rounded the corner, coffee in hand, aw-shucks smirk on his puffy face. Seeing me, he paused to hitch his pants higher, wiggling the belt around his paunch. He tried to look serious as he strode forward with renewed, big-boy purpose.

Never would get used to seeing Turley in his police uniform. Back in high school, that guy dropped more acid than anyone I knew. We used to throw huge parties up at Coal Creek Reservoir. I'm talking four, five kegs, bonfires, boom boxes, the kind of parties that would last three days and wouldn't end until everyone had puked at least once. I remember at one of these parties, Turley was tripping so hard he thought he was an alligator and dove into the reservoir, snapping his teeth and trying to catch invisible fish. This was in the early thaw of spring; water had to be forty degrees. Would've frozen to death if a couple guys from Longmont hadn't jumped in and dragged his fat ass out. He lay on the shore as they tried wrapping him in a blanket, flopping hysterically, his big, white belly pale as the underside of a toad in the harvest moonlight. Now, here he was, one of Ashton's finest.

He stuck out his hand with pretentious formality. When I didn't return the gesture, he slung an arm around my shoulder instead, like my reluctance to touch him had been an invitation for more intimacy. He kept his arm there, pulling me awkwardly closer, luring me down the hall with him.

"Claire," he said over his shoulder, a little too loudly, "I'll be down in Interrogation Room 1 if you need me."

Turley ushered me into a cramped space reminiscent of a small high school classroom. There was even a TV and a DVD player sitting on a rolling cart, the kind you used to be thrilled to see in science or history class because it meant a day of doing nothing. I could picture Turley and the rest of Ashton's tiny force huddled around endless hours of "Amphetamines and You" educational videos, as Sheriff Pat Sumner drew up strategies on the EZ Erase board to combat underage drinking at the strip mall with the simplified Xs and Os of a peewee squad's limited playbook.

"Can I get you something?" he asked. "Coffee?"

"No."

"Tom tell you I called?"

"Why else would I be here, Turley?"

He shifted in his seat and propped up straighter, wiping his expression of any lingering familiarity. I could appreciate what he was trying to do. But it's hard to take someone seriously after you've seen him pretending to be an alligator in his tidy whities.

"Got him cooling in a cell," Turley said, jabbing a thumb backward. "Didn't know what else to do."

"Drugs?" I asked, matter-of-factly.

"Not this time," Turley said, reaching for his Styrofoam cup. "I mean, I'm sure he's gacked to the gills. Your brother usually is."

The fluorescents buzzed overhead.

"Why'd you pick him up then?"

Turley's face twisted up.

"Spit it out, man."

Turley exhaled, rubbing the back of his meaty neck. "Your brother got in a fight with his business partner. Now, the guy ain't been home for a couple days. His mama called us this afternoon, freaking out. Chris was shooting off at the mouth. Made some threats, I guess. Pat had me pick him up, see if I could get to the bottom of it. Found Chris at the Arby's, sitting curbside, no jacket. Had to be fifteen degrees out—"

"Wait a second. Hold on. What business partner?"

"Pete." Turley waited for a reaction. "Pete Naginis?"

I returned a blank stare.

"Don't you talk to your brother no more?"

"Of course I talk to him. He's my brother. But I don't know anything about any business *or* partner."

The truth was, I avoided Chris as best I could. I insisted he check in periodically with a phone call. A short, to-the-point phone call. Thanks for letting me know that you haven't OD'd. No, you can't have any money. Bye. We didn't get too deep. Still, I found it difficult to believe he could've gotten his shit together enough to start a business. At least one that didn't involve drugs.

"Chris and Pete have a used computer store," Turley said, when it became obvious he needed to fill in the blanks. "Computer Solutions. Run it out of the old Chinese restaurant on the Desmond Turnpike."

"Don't know it."

"Yeah, you do. Way north. Just before Coal Creek. Red building, after that used car lot where they install those inflatable wacky wavers on weekends. No one ever admitted eating there except Woody Morris, and we used to bust his balls for it. Remember? There was that big joke about how all the town's strays had gone missing, and then the health department closed them down that one time because they found out it was true. It's on the way to the reservoir. Passed it a hundred times. You know it."

"I don't. But, whatever." I tried to wrap my brain around this. A business? "What exactly do they do at this shop?" I couldn't picture my brother as an entrepreneur. Or see him associating with anyone that upstanding. I knew Chris and his junkie buddies were into that cyber crap, video games or whatever, but broke-ass derelicts who skate between couches and homelessness aren't nabbing primo interest rates on small business loans.

"Trade, sell. Used crap. Busted stereos, tape decks, speakers. Old electronics. Most of their business is e-recycling."

"E-recycling?"

"I don't know much about that egghead stuff, Jay. Way I understand it, people drop off their old computers and Chris and Pete throw them away for them."

"Why would you pay someone to throw away your computer for you? Just dump it in a goddamn trash can."

Turley shrugged.

"Chris doesn't have any money." Collection agencies call my number all the time trying to get paid. "How did my brother get anyone to rent him a space?"

"Lease is in Betty Naginis' name," said Turley, slurping his coffee. "Pete's mom."

"Listen, I've been working all day. I'm tired as shit. I'd like to pop by Jenny's and say good night to my kid. I don't know any Pete. Or where he is. Ask my brother."

"I tried. He just goes on and on about some conspiracy and how we're all in on it. One minute he's going off about Pete, the next, Gerry Lombardi and the wrestling team."

"He's had a thorn up his ass about Mr. Lombardi for twenty years."

"Then he was shouting about you."

"What about me?"

"I don't know, man. I'm telling you, he wasn't making any sense. Talking a mile a minute, eyes bugging out his skull, arms flailing like a drunk monkey. Y'know when someone presents a danger to himself or others, I have the obligation to lock him up."

"My brother's nuts. Three years ago he was convinced he had Ebola. Last spring he cut up Jenny's *People* magazine to show how freemasons run Hollywood. He's bat-shit crazy."

"Trust me, I'm used to your brother's antics. Normally, I'd let him sober up, send him on his way. But it's different this time. A man is missing."

"Forty-year-old junkies sometimes don't come home to their mamas. Don't act like this is something more than it is."

"He was overheard threatening to kill the guy."

"When?"

"Up at the Naginis house. Couple days ago. I guess Betty lets Chris crash there from time to time. Use the shower and stuff. She said him and her son got into a real knock-down, drag-out fight, and that when she finally managed to pull them apart, Chris leveled some serious threats."

"What'd he say, exactly?"

"Y'know, Jay, the usual. 'You do that and you'll be sorry,' 'You're a dead man,' etcetera."

"In other words, the hotheaded, irrational shit people say when they have an argument."

"Sure," Turley said. "But your brother isn't just anybody. He's got some history."

I narrowed my eyes. "You better not be going where I think you are."

"Cool your jets."

"Then what was that crack about?"

"It wasn't a crack." He stared pleadingly. "Please. Sit back. Relax."

I sat back. But I wasn't relaxed.

"Jay, I known you a long time."

"Don't you forget it."

"But I have a job, okay? And I have bosses. This isn't some party by the reservoir. We're all grown-ups here." He showed his palms in mock surrender. "Let's put the cards on the table, okay? Mano a mano."

"What cards?"

"The brake line of your folks' car was tampered with."

I narrowed my eyes before waving an arm over the tiny room. "You may be able to strut around here, Turley, with your big dick-swinging cop routine, but I seen you with your pants off, with your underwear around your head and you playing a drunken fool, and you got a needle dick."

"I'm a real cop, Jay. I passed my exams. They gave me the job. So you don't have a choice. You've got to show me some respect."

"Fuck, I do." I gnashed my teeth. "My parents drove off a bridge and drowned. Twenty years ago. You were eight years old. You don't re-member jack."

"We have files. And I'm not the only one who—"

"Drop this small-town innuendo bullshit. I'm tired of it. It's old, unfounded news. If there had been any evidence, they would've arrested my brother and sent him away a long time ago. But they didn't. Never even charged him. It's only an issue now because assholes like you who weren't even there keep bringing it up like a bunch of harpy housewives."

"Now hold on, Jay—"

"And I'll tell you something else, Turley. Murderers have motives. Murderers have something to gain. My brother and I lost everything the night our folks died. We lost our house, we lost our money. Chris practi-cally turned into a junkie overnight, and has been living on the street ever since. So don't come to me now pretending to be a real cop out to solve some big mystery. Go issue your traffic citations and eat your donuts, or whatever the fuck they pay you to do. My brother may be a lying scumbag, but he's not a killer. I'm sick of people like you implying he had anything to do with them dying. It's disrespectful to me. And to my brother. And to my parents' memory. And I'll tell you something else—you listening to me?"

"Yeah, I'm listening, Jay."

"Next time you make a crack like that, you'd better be sure there's room in that cell for me too."

Turley nodded.

"Now, you plan on charging Chris with something?"

"He hasn't—I mean—" He stopped and shook his head no.

"Then I'd like to take my brother home."

* * *

"I thought you were coming by," Jenny said. I couldn't discern whether the mournful tone in her voice was disgust or disappointment.

I stood in front of the station, under the awning, smoking a cigarette. Intermittently, I'd clomp my boots or blow on my hands, anything to keep the blood flowing. Snow continued to fall—the forecast called for half a foot—temperatures plummeting into single digits. I was still seething. But I made sure to keep calm with Jenny. Anytime I got high strung, her hackles got up, and that never ended well.

"I'm sorry," I said. "I wanted to come by. Give Aiden a big kiss for me."

"He's already asleep." Jenny paused. I could hear her working words over in her mind, trying to construct the exact phrase that would cut me the most. One of those fucked-up parts of loving someone. You know the other's greatest weakness. Instead of doing what you can to protect wounds, you wait for the most opportune times to exploit them.

"I don't understand you," she said. "You talk about wanting to spend more time with your son, and all you do is find new ways to let us down."

"I *do* want to spend more time with him. And with you. I miss you both."

There was a long silence on the other end of the line. I thought she might actually say something encouraging. Then I heard a door slam on her end and Brody grumbling. Jenny must've told him it was me on the phone, because the grumbling continued, but the inflection changed.

Turley poked his head out the door into the cold. "He's all ready."

"Who's ready?" Jenny asked.

"Nothing."

"Who was that? Where are you?"

"The police station."

"Chris?"

"Yeah." I knew I'd just hand delivered her the invitation she needed to tear me a new asshole. Half our fights were over Chris and what she saw as my coddling him. I was hardly the guy's biggest fan these days, but you can't let people take a shit on your brother, no matter how big a bastard he is. So I braced for what was coming next. Only, nothing did. Then I realized her silence was actually worse. You don't waste your time talking when you've given up trying. I did the same damn thing with my brother. When I stopped bitching and got off his back, it wasn't because I was suddenly cool with his fucked-up lifestyle; I just didn't give a shit anymore. And it sucked being on the receiving end of that ambivalence.

"I'll stop by tomorrow morning, Jenny. Promise. It's Saturday, I don't have any work. Maybe we can—"

"Okay, Jay," she said.

"I have some money for you too."

But she'd already hung up.

CHAPTER THREE

We bounced along old country roads in my battered Chevy without talking. Strapped with a ratty, brown backpack in which he carted his world, Chris had bummed a smoke when he first climbed in, but hadn't spoken a word since. He looked like shit. I'd expected him to look bad; somehow, he looked even worse than that. Half his head was sheared in a bleached-out, homemade haircut, with crusted bloody slits around the ears, like he'd used glass shards for scissors and a toaster for a mirror. In the dim, blue-gray light of the cab, he resembled a cadaver, waxy, colorless flesh drawn tightly over protruding bone. His eyes, two vacuous pits, sat deep in the sockets with giant black rings around them, and his badly neglected teeth stuck out. When he sucked on his cigarette, he pulled so hard, you'd think his eyeballs might disappear straight through the back of his head and the whole thing would instantly turn to ash.

In the five or six months since I'd seen him last, he appeared to have lost weight. I'd seen cancer patients with more meat on their bones. Over six feet, he couldn't have weighed more than a buck forty. Despite the long time apart, I felt no joy in our reunion. I'm pretty sure the feeling was mutual. We were brothers, blood on blood, and that counts for something. There had been a time, right after the accident, when we might've been close. But those days were long behind us now.

I steered up Axel Rod Road, past Tyne Machinery, where our father had worked. I could still recall the horror stories he'd tell. Hot solvents scarring the skin, limbs caught in gears, a Gothic novel nightmare. The factory used to employ half of Ashton, but went under years ago. Literally. The building had been abandoned so long that the crumbling

structure was sinking back into the earth. Crooked trees and unruly veg-
etation fastened onto the frame. Roots and weeds erupted from hard
soil, sprawling up through the cracks, coiling around anchors and joists,
latching onto studs and roof beams. Each time I passed the cracked
foundation and shattered glass, I'd think of the tremendous sacrifices
our father had made to give us a good home. Which, in turn, would
only make me feel like a bigger bastard for not being able to do that for
my son.

I glanced over at my brother. Chris didn't have a coat. He wore the
same threadbare T-shirt he always did, dark blue with a pair of faded
cherries, from the old Pac-Man arcade game. Every time I saw him he
was wearing it. What kind of life do you lead where you only own one
T-shirt? His dirty jeans, coated in a slick, greasy sheen, stank like rank
cheese and gasoline. With the heater in my truck not working, Chris
must've been freezing his balls off—I was bundled in layers and could
barely keep from shivering. I'd asked him a couple times if he wanted
my coat, but he shook me off. I'm sure he'd been outside in worse.

Nothing but static on the radio, which was normal for these parts.
CD player was broken and only made a clacking sound when you stuck
in a disc. I had a new stereo Tom had given me, still in the box, shrink-
wrapped and everything, but I hadn't bothered opening the package.
Which sucked, because I kept my entire music collection in the truck.
Anytime I was in the mood for some tunes, stuck fruitlessly twiddling
the knob, I'd gaze down at all the music I couldn't play, and it only
served as a reminder that I couldn't get my act together.

Usually, I didn't mind the quiet, but tonight, sitting next to my
brother, the silence only amplified the distance between us.

The roads hadn't been plowed, and the town wouldn't send out
trucks until the storm calmed. Couldn't go faster than fifteen miles an
hour or I'd fishtail into a culvert.

"Where we going?" Chris finally asked.

"My place, I guess. Unless you have somewhere else you need to
be." It was a dick thing to say, since we both knew he didn't. As much
as he disgusted me at that moment, I wasn't kicking my brother out to
roam dark, snowy streets in a T-shirt. I didn't know where he slept most

nights. The bus station in Longmont? The Y on Kirby? One of the mo-tels on the Turnpike? A crack den? No fucking idea. This was my flesh-and-blood brother sitting next to me, and the reality of his life was as graspable to me as ether.

Following Turley's story down at the jail, I'd been anticipating non-stop conspiracy theories and antigovernment gibberish about all the ways the authorities were out to screw Chris. Which was a recurring theme in my brother's life. Because it was always about him. It was pathetic how Chris tried to inject relevance into his existence this way. He didn't un-derstand that he was inconsequential, didn't matter; that he was expend-able. They could find my brother frozen beneath a tree in a park or with a needle in his arm in some skid row room, as they most certainly would someday, and nobody's life would be impacted. Not even mine. In my more honest moments, I'd have to admit, if to no one but myself, that any sorrow I might feel for this loss would immediately be offset by the tre-mendous sense of relief.

Hank Miller had closed up the station already, so the tiny lot was pitch black. I parked my truck behind the squat brick garage, and made for the small apartment above it. This is where I'd lived for over a de-cade. What's that? One-eighth of my life? Maybe more, depending on if I get cut down as early as my folks. Never really thought about it that way. Certainly hadn't envisioned a future here when I rented the place just out of high school, but that's what it became. My future. Like ev-erything else in my life, a temporary plan that had turned permanent. My job with Tom. My situation with Jenny. My less than stellar start to fatherhood. Someday, it would all change. Someday, I would make it right. Only someday never comes, does it? I'd been in this same shithole for ten years. Three different women had lived there with me, including the mother of my kid, but, in the end, I always ended up alone.

I usually had a decent outlook on life, but anytime I hung around Chris, this is what happened. Another reason I avoided the guy. Noth-ing good ever came of it. I never walked away from seeing my brother, saying, "Gee, sure glad I did that." His mere presence could put me in a funk that would last for days. Not to mention all the trouble he had caused in my relationship with Jenny.

I remembered the night she left, the night she packed up our son and moved out on me. I couldn't shake the scene. Pissing rain pelting the roof. Aiden wailing in his car seat carrier. Tears streaming down her face as she pleaded with me to believe her.

Chris had stolen some pills from her purse, painkillers the doctor had prescribed following the birth. Just a few pills that she never touched but always knew were there. Until they weren't. My brother had stopped by under the pretense of wanting to see his nephew and, somehow, he'd sniffed them out, snatched them from under our noses. Because if there was an unattended narcotic within a fifty-mile radius, Chris could zero in on that shit like a 'roided-up bloodhound.

Instead of calling out my brother like I should have, I abandoned Jenny in her accusation. Chris swore on our parents' life that he hadn't taken the pills, and, even though I knew he was lying, I backed him up anyway. That fight was about more than the pills. That night Jenny had needed me to take a side. And I did. I just picked the wrong one.

The light, a single, uncovered bulb, blazed in the narrow well leading upstairs. Creaking wood stretched and groaned, the hollow, winding winds rattling the whole decrepit building.

I unlocked the front door, which led into my tiny kitchen, Chris right on my heels, before he pushed past me like it was somehow his apartment too. I threw my keys on the table, next to the stack of red-letter bills I'd been ignoring.

"Got any beer?" Chris asked, dropping his backpack that reeked of bum shit on the same kitchen table where I ate.

I walked by him into the TV room. "Check the fridge." I flicked on the television, searching for the Bruins game.

My nameless cat scratched on the porch. I didn't even know how it became *my* cat. Belonged to the neighbors, I think, but it kept coming around. So I pet it, fed it. I'd wake in the middle of the night and somehow the fat thing would've scaled the drainpipe and I'd find her stuck on my second-floor landing, crying to be let in. This is what you get for being a nice guy. One day, I look out and the neighbors are gone, house boarded up with a "For Sale" sign, and now I'm stuck with the damn thing. That was over a year ago. Never got around to naming it. I'm not too philosophical a guy, don't like to get too heavy, but it was hard not to draw a correlation. I mean, I couldn't even name the fucking cat I'd been feeding and taking care of for over a year because I didn't want to get too attached.

My brother stood in the doorway, rail-thin arms up in a *T* over the frame, hanging there like a crucified, junkie Jesus. "No beer in the fridge, little brother."

"Then I'm fucking out, Chris."

The Bruins were down three with four minutes left, the Devils on a power play. I switched it off and dropped in the chair and pulled my fingers through my hair.

"Got any money?" he asked. "I'll run downstairs and grab us some."

You hand my brother money, and that's the last you'll see of him. He'd trade the warmth of a bed indoors for the chance to get high, every time.

Chris dropped from the frame and slinked over to the couch, wiry body shiftless as an underfed snake in a windblown field. He snared my cigarettes from the table, flicking a match and inhaling deeply, sinking into the sofa, whose stuffed cushions threatened to devour him.

"You going to tell me what that shit was about tonight?" I asked.

Chris gazed over expressionless, like he didn't have a clue what I was talking about.

"Tonight. At the station. Where I was dragged down after a long day of work."

Chris dismissively waved a hand.

"Turley said you've been getting in fights—making threats. What the hell is wrong with you?"

"Fuck Rob Turley. I remember catching that tub of lard huffing paint thinner behind the Community Center. Now he wants to act like a big dick-swinging cop."

I swiped the Marlboro Lights off the arm of the couch. "I think there's some beer under the sink. Grab me one too."

My brother brushed the wisps of peroxide blond back into that cockamamie homemade haircut and bounced up gleefully.

"Stick the rest in the fridge," I called out.

I felt the money Tom had given me in my pocket. I ran through the math in my head. The envelope, plus what I'd managed to save these past few weeks, minus rent, bills, gas, food, I had enough to catch up with what I owed Jenny. Wouldn't leave me much afterward. But Tom always had work for me, sooner or later. Question was, if it wasn't soon, would I be able to hold out till later? It was a bad habit of mine. Whenever I got stressed, I insisted on making matters worse by mulling over finances. Working for Tom, I knew I wouldn't starve or be homeless, but I sure as shit wasn't getting ahead either. I'd never own my own house or be able to afford a vehicle that wasn't used. I'd never have enough to squirrel away something for Aiden's college fund, and even though that last one was a long ways off, the day would come eventually.

Chris handed me a beer, smiling. "Like ol' times, eh?" He flashed his country yellow teeth.

"You look like shit," I said. "When was the last time you saw a dentist?"

Chris peeled back his lips with grubby fingers. You could see black rot eating into the roots.

"It isn't funny," I said. "You're going to need a root canal. Make an appointment with Dr. Johnson. Get a goddamn cleaning, at least. Have him send me the bill."

My brother grunted that he would, though I knew he had no intention of seeing our old family dentist ever again. He tipped back the beer and sat on the arm of the couch, arcing his core forward like some yoga pose I once saw Jenny do when she was trying to lose the baby weight, not that she was ever bigger than a peanut.

Chris stared intently at the TV, as if despite its being turned off he could still see some riveting narrative unfold beyond the black glass.

"Turley says you've gone into business with a partner. You opened, what, a computer removal company?"

"Electronic waste," Chris said. "E-recycling. You know how good Pete is with computers."

"Sure," I said, even though I didn't know who the hell Pete was. Might've been this skateboarder dude with kinky hair and glasses I'd met once. Maybe not. What difference would it have made? All these losers he ran with were the same to me. Some were shorter, fatter, darker; some had longer hair, better teeth. Didn't faze me. I glossed over their existence the way you do the boring parts of a book.

"Aw, you don't give a shit," Chris said.

"No, not really." I sucked at the warm suds. "But I *do* want to know why I had to go down to the station and bail your ass out. You fucked up my entire evening."

"You didn't have to put up bail."

"I meant figuratively. I was supposed to see Aiden tonight."

"Yeah? How is my nephew?"

"I wouldn't know, Chris. I didn't get to see him. I was stuck listening to Turley do his impression of a big city cop, rehashing shit that happened a hundred years ago because, apparently, you've been running off at the mouth and threatening to kill people. Now, do you know where this Pete is? Where he hangs out? There's my phone. Make some calls to your buddies because his mother is worried."

"You remember that summer we spent at the shore in Rhode Island?" Chris asked.

"Huh?"

"We went with Aunt Dee Dee and Uncle Chip, Mom, Dad. You were real little. Four, five. You remember that?" The fat, unnamed cat lay curled next to my brother, who stroked her absentmindedly, tufts of fluffy white fur coming off by the fistfuls.

"I don't know. Maybe. We went more than once." I had vague recollections of the ocean, gathering shells on a beach, filling buckets with wet sand to make castles. Early childhood, fuzzy memories. I knew my folks rented a cottage down there with my aunt and uncle a couple summers. I had pictures in an album somewhere. We stopped making the long trek a few years before the accident.

"Our place was right on the beach, fifty yards from the water." He didn't look at me when he said this, his voice subdued, laid-back, as if the beer was really relaxing him. Except that it had been a while since a single beer had had that kind of effect on my brother.

"You almost drowned," he said.

"No, I didn't. When?"

"It was at night," he continued, still not looking at me. "The Din-das—they rented the place next door—had stopped by. There was a par-ty in the kitchen, everyone drinking, music playing. Mom had gone to bed with a headache. You wandered down to the beach, waded in. An undertow pulled you out, dragging you far, far from the shore."

"You're making that up. I don't remember anything like that. Where was Dad?"

Chris nursed his beer, shrugged.

"How am I still here then? I couldn't swim when I was five. Why didn't I drown?"

"I had hooked up with Jody White." His voiced droned as if in a trance, just another story told to a stranger at closing time. "God, I liked her. She was this tasty blonde-haired doll. Teeny, high voice. Swear if you stuck a finger in her, she'd squeak. Family had a cottage up the road. We were in her room, her parents out somewhere. I had my hand up her shirt. She was one of those pristine Catholic girls, so it was a big deal just getting to second base. Perfect sixteen-year-old tits." He sighed with fond remembrance. "And I stopped. I knew something was wrong. Felt it right here—" Chris poked a scarecrow finger into his bony sternum. "Didn't say a word to Jody. Just hopped up and bolted out the door, ran all the way down the beach. I instinctively knew to go to the water. I don't know how I knew. But I did. It was like I could hear you scream-ing. In my head. Nobody could hear you a stone's throw from the cot-tage. But I could hear you. Half a mile away. I dove in the water and pulled you out."

It was perfectly still for a moment.

Then Chris took another glug of beer and belched loudly.

"A regular fucking Superman," I said.

It's funny when people start talking about things that happened to you before you can really remember them. It's like their stories worm memories into your brain. I certainly didn't recall almost drowning, and I'd never heard my parents mention it, but after he said that I started to get pictures in my mind's eye of swirling black water, felt the shivers of panic and desperation, tasted the thick salt clogging my throat as consciousness slipped away. Then I saw a hand reach down in the murky depths and hoist me up into the clear, clean moonlight.

Suggestion is a powerful thing.

"Did that really happen?" I asked.

"I don't know," he mumbled. "Maybe."

Chris got up and went to the window, peering out into the swirling snow as though trying to locate something precious in the abyss.

He stood there a long time, T-shirt draped off his bony frame as if it was a wire coat hanger.

"I tell you something," he said. "You got to keep it under wraps, okay?"

"Sure." Who the fuck would I tell?

"Pete and me, well, Pete mostly—he's a whiz with computers—so we got this business on the side." He peered over his shoulder. "Electronic recycling." He enunciated the words clearly, since he knew he was talking a different language. "Disposing of old hard drives, smartphones, anything with digital data, that kind of shit."

"And people *pay* you for this?"

"Fuck, yeah, man. You can't throw that shit in the *garbage*."

"Why not?"

He looked at me as if I was missing half a head.

"Because it's got, like, all your personal information on there, little brother. Your computer is as personalized as a goddamn fingerprint these days. You'd know this if you joined the rest of the twenty-first century."

Coming from a homeless junkie, that stung. But I had to admit he was right; I didn't know jack about computers. I wasn't big on technology, period. Honestly, if it wasn't for Jenny pressing me, I probably wouldn't even have gotten a cell phone, not that it matters up here; half the calls get dropped anyway. I don't like being plugged in to someone's beck and call. I didn't own a computer. Rarely used the Internet for anything. Didn't even have an email address. At least not one I ever checked. I didn't have time to sit on my ass playing video games or ogling pictures of naked women. I was too busy busting my ass to keep my head above water.

I could picture this business of his. A gang of pasty dope fiends gacking over circuit boards and Legend of Zelda, or whatever nerds played these days. I supposed I should've applauded his initiative, told him I was proud of him for at least trying, provided positive feedback, but I couldn't muster the enthusiasm. It was too late in the game, especially when I knew feeding the habit comes first, and that its appetite is insatiable. So what did it matter? Whatever ambition my brother had shown wouldn't last long; it'd be up with the smoke he inhaled to get high. You can't have a life when you are on drugs. Because being on drugs *is* your life.

A truck outside backfired, and my brother practically jumped out of his ragged old kicks.

He caught me laughing.

"What's so funny?"

"Nothing," I said. "I'm glad you've started a company, a business, whatever you and Pete are doing. Really. It's terrific."

He turned around and faced me, eyes glassed over as he tongued a scab on the corner of his blistered lips.

"But you didn't help your cause with Turley down at the station. Guy's just trying to help out some old woman who's worried about her son. You should know you're only going to make it worse by carrying on like a lunatic. Everyone knows you around here. Just being high is against the law. Turley and Pat Sumner can lock you up for that. All they need to do is draw your blood. How long you think you'd last in a real prison?"

"We found something, Jay."

"What do you mean, 'you found something'?"

"Someone dropped off a computer. We were cleaning the hard drive. That's what we do. Erase the hard drive, remove old files, data, pictures. We—found something."

"Erase?" I started to get it. "You mean you go rooting around for personal information you can use." I might not have known a lot about computers, but I wasn't stupid. Phony credit cards were a billion dollar industry.

Chris smirked.

"Jesus Christ," I said, pushing myself up.

"Sure, sometimes we have a look around. What's the big deal? They're throwing the things away. What are you getting all pissed off for?"

"Because people are trusting you to do a job. I know that word doesn't mean anything to you. But it's how the rest of the world operates. And you are taking advantage of them. Identity theft? That's what you're into these days, Chris?"

You'd have to be an idiot to drop off a computer to my brother and his junkie pals.

He wet his lips, bobbing like a madman, crazy eyes bugging again. "You're missing my point. We uncovered something. It's big, man."

"What? Someone's bank statement?"

"Ain't no bank statement, little brother. I mean, big. *Really big.* What we found is going to *rock* this town. I'm talking shake this fucker to the core!" He pointed frantically at his pigeon chest. "Gonna see I was right all along. Gonna see—"

I'd had enough. Given my brother's refusal to appreciate the gravity of his situation, I didn't see the point in humoring his persecution fantasies or delusions of grandeur any longer. If he wasn't going to take his life seriously, why should I?

I patted him on the back. "Okay, Sam Spade. Blankets are in the closet there. Take the couch. Get some sleep. There's nothing here worth stealing, and if I find something missing in the morning, I swear to fucking God, Chris, it'll be the last time I ever let you inside."

My brother grabbed my wrist.

The soft light of the room yellowed his flesh like greasy chicken skin.

"What?"

He dropped his voice to a whisper. "You need to hear what I have to say."

"I'm listening."

"You sure you can keep a secret?"

"Yeah, Chris. I can keep a secret. But I don't have time to play make-believe. I'm a grown-ass man with grown-up shit to do. So either tell me what that bullshit at the station was really about or—"

"It's big, little brother. Real big."

"Jesus Christ! Tell me, already."

Chris looked out the corners of his eyes, held a finger to his lips, and beckoned me nearer.

I leaned in, my ear right next to his mouth, so close I could feel his hot breath.

"I shot the sheriff," he whispered. "But I did not shoot the deputy."

Chris let go my wrist and hurled himself back onto the sofa, howling. About knocked himself out with that one. "But I swear it was in self-defense!" He was barely able to get the words out through the guffawing.

"You're an asshole."

"Come back, little brother. I was kidding. Where you going?"

"To bed. See you in the morning."

"I'm serious. We really did find something. Don't you want to know what it is?"

"No. I don't." I slammed shut my bedroom door.

When I woke in the morning, he was gone.

CHAPTER FOUR

I let my truck idle while I scraped the ice from my windshield. The bright morning sun rose over the crest of Lamentation Mountain, splashing orange splotches through snow-covered birches, halos ringing between tall evergreen trees. The news put the damage at over a foot, considerably worse than the original forecast. They were calling for an even bigger storm to roll in next week, a real Nor'easter. Trace flurries drifted down, floating aimlessly, catching the glint of the sun's rays. I watched my breath crystalize in front of me.

I pulled around the front of Hank's to fill up. Would run me close to sixty-five dollars, thing sucked so much gas. The floor of my cab was littered with crinkled receipts and stiff papers, empty coffee cups and crushed cigarette packs, Gatorade bottles, fast food bags; the inside of my ride looked like a refugee camp. Waiting for the pump to stop, I gathered all the junk and threw it away. Doesn't seem like much, but I felt like I accomplished something. Jenny was always complaining about what a slob I was.

Went inside to grab a coffee and a copy of the *Herald*, even though I seldom read the damn thing these days. I used to be up on the latest news; now I bought the paper mostly out of habit. A high school kid took my money. He was wearing an Ashton Redcoats varsity wrestling jacket, so we shot the shit about that for a few. He said they were leaving for Regionals tomorrow. I told him about the year my brother and Adam Lombardi won the State Championship. He said, "Cool," but to him I was probably just an old guy reliving his glory days. And not even *my* glory days, but my piece-of-shit junkie brother's. I couldn't fathom thirty when I was seventeen.

* * *

Back on the road, I was able to dial in the classic rock station, 105, The Bone. The Outfield's "Your Love" came on. Always made me smile. We never settled on an official song, but I used to tease Jenny that was it, and I'd belt it out when I wanted to mess with her. Used to piss her off since the song is about the singer's girlfriend, "Jenny," being on a vacation far away, and him screwing around with another, younger girl. Jenny wouldn't really get mad, though, more like fake mad. She knew I only teased her when I was in a good mood.

I blasted the tune, which crackled in and out through the static, as I fired up the day's first cigarette and the caffeine started to kick in, sunbeams smacking the snow and ice that coated my hometown. I rolled down the window and let the cold, brisk mountain air wash over me. Pulled down the visor and strapped on my sunglasses, let the cigarette dangle from my lips, and cranked the radio up louder. You take your small victories wherever you can find them.

Jenny's place was past the trestles in the center of town, above the same bar and grill where she worked nights, The Landover. A dumpy two-bedroom, it wasn't much nicer than mine. The proximity to her job was convenient, since Aiden was just upstairs and she could pop in and check on him during breaks. Her boyfriend, Brody, worked second shift at the die shop, so it's not like Aiden was alone long.

Early Saturday morning, most people still in bed following the storm, the streets empty, nothing open yet besides the Dunkin' Donuts and gas stations, the town perfectly peaceful, I tooled freshly plowed streets, tapping out a beat on the dash and feeling pretty damn all right. I didn't give my brother another thought. Which was how I'd managed to deal with him all these years. Out of sight, out of mind.

On weekends when I was a kid, my dad would go into town for his morning paper and bring us back a dozen donuts. A time-honored tradition. It was time I started building memories like that for Aiden. I flipped a bitch and circled back to the Dunkin' Donuts.

* * *

"You know I don't want him eating sugar," Jenny said, snatching the box from me.

"One donut won't kill him."

"No, it won't. But refined sugar is not good for his development. It's been linked to depression."

"Depression? He's not even two yet. Where'd you hear that?"

"In the baby books. You should try reading one sometime."

"Enough shit hasn't gone wrong for him to be depressed yet."

"Fine. But I still don't want to have to deal with a hyperactive child all day."

"You don't have to. I thought I could bundle him up, take him down to the Little People's Playground, play in the snow a bit."

"Fine," she said again, "but I *still* don't want him eating sugar."

"Fine," I said, mimicking her, prying the box from her hands and flipping open the top. "You eat them then."

She wrinkled her nose. "Like I can eat a donut."

I grabbed a plump, powdered jelly, moving toward her. "Open up. You're looking pretty damn thin."

Jenny flushed and started backing up, lips cracking a smile. She'd answered the door in an old Pink Floyd T-shirt of mine, sleep-tossed hair, those long legs showing underneath, so smooth and touchable, bare feet tiptoeing on linoleum. This was when she looked best in my opinion, first thing in the morning, all rumpled, no makeup, no fuss, just-rolled-out-of-bed, perfect.

"Come on, Jenny. One bite." I cocked my arm.

She started batting at me. "Knock it off, Jay," she said, trying to look stern, but giggling. "I mean it."

I had her retreated in the corner, pretending I was going to force-feed a jelly donut like those obnoxious couples do with wedding cake. I was kidding, of course, but I got her laughing so hard she couldn't breathe. Which made me start to laugh too.

I dipped and darted like I planned to grab her waist and pull her in, but she jerked away and slapped my hand, then held a finger to her mouth and pointed at the bedroom door, which I took to mean that Brody was still asleep.

He'd walked in when we were on the phone last night when he should've been at work. Maybe he called in sick or was sleeping one off. Maybe he didn't work second shift anymore. What the hell did I care?

Hearing us carrying on, Aiden came running out of the living room.

"Da da! Da da!"

With his shaggy brown hair and big brown eyes, he looked just like his mother. Jenny reprimanded him to be quiet. But I didn't give a damn if we disrupted Brody's sleep. I scooped him up and hoisted him high, gave him a big squeeze and then lifted his shirt for a belly fart. I didn't need any baby book to tell me belly farts always made a kid laugh. It's like Dad 101.

As soon as I set him down, Aiden grabbed my finger and dragged me into the living room, where his mother had him set up with breakfast—scrambled eggs and sausage cut into extra tiny pieces—which he'd slopped all over the carpet in front of the TV.

"Oh, sugar's bad," I teased her, "but TV's okay?"

"You try watching him without a distraction once in a while." She flashed a pained smirk. "Especially when Mommy drank too much last night."

I slowly shook my head, feigning disappointment. "Since when do you drink so much you're hungover?"

"When you don't do it often, trust me, it doesn't take much."

Aiden yanked my hand to sit down and watch cartoons, which weren't at all like the cartoons I remembered. I grew up with the classics. Tom and Jerry. Bugs Bunny. Popeye. Actual cartoons. These were done by a computer or something. Everything was computers these days. God, I hated the damn things. Not that my view on the subject mattered to Aiden; these were the only cartoons he'd ever known, and he was transfixed, fuzzy glow from the screen flickering over his tiny features, eyes entranced, lit up wide.

I turned back. Jenny hovered over us. She had a big smile on her face. I was lying there, cockeyed, unable to get up or even make myself more comfortable because my boy wanted me there like that, and anytime I tried to move, he'd start shouting, "Down down," which made Jenny tell him to be quiet or he'd wake up Brody, which caused me to laugh, and Jenny said to stop because it was only encouraging him to be bratty, but she was laughing a little too.

"What the hell's going on?" Brody asked, rubbing his eyes. He stood shirtless. Badly drawn tattoos adorned his shoulders and flanks. The long hair that he usually had tied off in a ponytail hung loose, framing his sharp, angular features, face coated in scruff. "I'm trying to sleep." Then he saw me. "Oh, hey, Jay. Didn't know you was here." He said it nice as he could, considering we'd just woken him up.

Brody snagged his smokes off the table, but before he could light one, Jenny shot him a look. He dropped the pack and crept up behind her, throwing his arms around her neck, kissing her as she squirmed. We locked eyes momentarily. Then he slunk back into the kitchen.

I pried myself from Aiden with a hair tousle and another promise I knew I wouldn't keep and followed them. Brody scratched himself under the old pair of blue jeans he had on. He flipped open the donuts, sifting through them like a fat secretary on hump day, selecting a chubby custard and clamping it in his teeth; a gob of cream squirted out the side. When he stretched over the stove for a box of cereal, I got a better look at some of those tattoos. The usual badass wannabe assortment of skulls and crosses, hula girls and she-devils. One in particular made me curious, though. A big black panther. Clearly a cover-up.

When Brody had hooked up with the mother of my kid, I'd felt compelled to dig around. I learned that he used to ride with a motorcycle club back in the day. I didn't know a lot about motorcycle clubs, but from what I understood they weren't something you could quit like a factory job. I would've been worried for Jenny and Aiden's safety had I not met the guy and thought he was such a tool. Plus, it's tough to base anything on small town rumors. The long hair and ink, the motorcycle and tough-guy posturing? I considered him to be more a cliché than the genuine article. Brody had stopped riding altogether after he slipped on a patch of ice last winter and broke a few ribs. I had a hunch that the big panther on his biceps might've been concealing the club's insignia, but I had no way of knowing for sure.

In the middle of the room, Jenny sat at the small, round kitchen table, hands cupped around a mug of coffee, which she kept blowing on even though no steam rose. She wouldn't look at me. Brody kept shooting me glances. I could tell something was up.

"What's going on?" I finally asked, after I'd had enough of the eyebrow twitching and panning back and forth.

"You tell him," Brody said, splashing milk into a giant bowl of Cap'n Crunch, practically tittering with smarminess.

"Tell me what?"

Jenny still wasn't looking at me. She wasn't looking at him, either. Instead, she stared out the window at a blue jay perched on a power line dripping icicles, and continued to blow on coffee that wasn't hot.

Brody shook his head with an overly familiar grin, as if suddenly we were part of the same fraternity of Man that women would never quite understand.

"Got me a foreman's job down in Rutland," he said. "Start in March."

"You're moving?"

I asked Jenny this, but Brody was the one who answered.

"Gonna look for a house down there," he said. "As in, like, *buy*." He leaned against the stove, slurping cereal like a twelve-year-old. "No more of this renting shit, Jay. Like pissing money down the drain, I'm tellin' ya. Get a house, pay that shit off, and then you actually *own* something, y'know? Get some equality. Something to call your own."

I didn't bother correcting the dumb shit that he meant "equity."

He pointed his spoon at me, milk dribbling down his chin. "That's how you do it," he said through a mumbled mouthful. "Ya hear me, bro?"

"When were you planning on telling me?" I asked her.

"I just found out," she said, finally turning my way.

Brody let go a laugh. "Stop busting his balls! I told her, like, a month ago."

"You said it was a *possibility*," Jenny said over her shoulder, lips curled in a mean snarl, a look I knew all too well. "You didn't tell me you actually *got* it till last night." She spun to shoot me that same mean glare. "And *you* didn't stop by until this morning, so you have no right."

Aiden came running in, tugging at my hand to go play with him some more, and it made me feel like an even bigger asshole to have to shoo him away, but my heart was thumping deep in my chest. He didn't need much encouragement; even little kids can tell when something isn't right.

Rutland was easily three, four hours away, and if I couldn't get over here now as often as I would've liked, with them just a couple miles down the road, when would I ever see my boy? Maybe it had been our own fault that Jenny and I couldn't work things out, but this was going to affect Aiden forever. I was his father, and she hadn't even told me. Instead, I'd had to suffer the indignity of hearing it from Brody.

Brody kept eyeing me, smirking as he slurped. It sounds weird, but despite the fact he was sleeping with my girl and helping to raise my kid, up until that point, I hadn't even thought enough of Brody to hate him. He wasn't a threat; he was just some dopey guy that Jenny was with because she didn't want to be alone. A rebound fuck.

Jenny stared up at me. She was still trying to look angry, but it wasn't working. The rims of her big brown eyes welled. I could see she wanted me to say something.

I pulled the envelope from my coat pocket and slapped it on the table. "That should catch me up," I said.

CHAPTER FIVE

The Little People's Playground sat perched on a hill next to the old police station, which had once been Ashton's elementary school back in the '50s, a dilapidated, brown brick building that now served as the town's Community Center, where they coordinated Easter egg hunts and sign-ups for youth sports. In the summer, we'd pedal our bicycles there and climb the hillside to a secret fort—an empty utility shed that had been gutted by a fire—where this squirrelly, cross-eyed kid, Arnie Perkins, stashed his father's old *Playboy* magazines in a rusted coffee tin. The fort was less than a football field away from the police station, tucked in the dense cover of musky New England foliage. We used to think we were so cool, real outlaws sitting up there, puffing away on stolen cigarettes, staring at dirty magazines as the late afternoon thunderheads would roll in.

Over the years, local businesses like McDonald's and Chester McGee's had donated old playground equipment to the park. There wasn't a lot for kids to do in Ashton. The nearest Chuck E. Cheese was three counties away. The LPP wasn't too exciting. Merry-go-round and teeter-totter, swing set, slide, a maze constructed from discarded tractor-trailer tires. I always enjoyed bringing Aiden there. I remembered my dad taking me when I was small. Felt like the memories I had of him faded by the day.

When we pulled up, there were so many kids there I thought they must've cancelled school. Then I remembered it was Saturday.

Trying not to let my stress affect Aiden, I did my best to remain upbeat, acting silly. A toddler doesn't need to see his dad falling apart. I'm the one who's supposed to have this shit figured out. On the way over we were singing nursery rhymes. I had him giggling, but honestly, that probably had more to do with the sugar from the lollipop I'd given him. His face was sticky with cherry. I kept a stash of candy in my glove compartment. His mother wouldn't approve, but she wasn't around, was she? And I wasn't one of those fathers who bought into all that new-age parenting bullshit. No sugar. No TV. A forced regimen from the crib through college. My parents didn't do that with us, and we turned out all right. Well, at least one of us did.

The snow that had fallen was the wet, heavy kind—perfect for snowballs and stacking—and several snowmen, in various states of construction, dotted the knoll. Two small boys, a few years older than Aiden, played on the merry-go-round, and he instantly gravitated to them. It's funny watching how cliques form, even at age two. The boys were bigger and therefore cooler, and Aiden wanted in with the "in" crowd. Trying to fit in with the cool kids would never change.

They were good with him, helping him up, not being too rough. I figured they probably had a little brother at home. I scanned the grounds for a parent, but didn't see one, which was hardly a surprise. Ashton, despite the squalor of the Turnpike and truck stop, was still the kind of town where you didn't have to lock your doors. Where you could forget your wallet on top of a gas pump at the Mobil station, and it'd be there when you went back. Where you didn't have to hover over your kids, and could let them be kids and play unsupervised in a park.

Watching Aiden play, I thought about the day he was born, seeing him for the first time, the overwhelming feelings that washed over me. I'd understood kids were an extension of you. Circle of life, *The Lion King* and all that. But that's not it. They're not an extension of you. They *are* you. Like, literally. I stared down at that tiny, squirming thing, crying and fussing, and when I looked in his eyes, I didn't see pieces of me, I saw me. Actually *me*. This newer, better, cleaner version who would now be running the race, and my sole job as a father was to make sure he had the tools to succeed.

Driving Jenny and our son home from the hospital, I was gung ho, up for the challenge, confident I could rise to the occasion like my dad had done. Only I didn't. I wasn't him. I couldn't get out of my own way.

No matter how hard I tried to go all in, something held me back, like a governor on a motorbike restricting full throttle. I couldn't put my finger on it. It wasn't a lack of love. I'd never loved anything so much in my whole life. But despite that love, I was unable to produce, which had made me feel like a failure.

"Cheer up. It's not that cold."

I craned my neck and saw Gerry Lombardi, Chris' old wrestling coach, looming behind me. Bundled in a North Face ski jacket and gloves, unruly gray eyebrows poking like brush bristles. Shiny cheeks and crinkling eyes, he smiled kindly. The guy was forever smiling. He had these big horse teeth that bucked out, which made him appear to always be happy. Hell, maybe he really was. A broad-shouldered man like his sons, but older now, with a chronic bad back and abysmal posture, Mr. Lombardi appeared to be shriveling, hunched over, like an old lady with a dowager hump.

With strained, creaking effort, Mr. Lombardi sat beside me, gazing over the playground.

He motioned to Aiden. "Getting big, eh? It's a fun age. I remember when Michael and Adam were that big. Just starting to find their way in the world, coming into their own, developing distinct personalities. Y'know, I could tell even then that Michael would go into some kind of public service."

I glanced over skeptically.

"No, it's true! The boy loved forms. When the UpStart kids would come by the house for pizza parties and sleepovers, Michael would make everyone fill out forms. A born bureaucrat."

"He was writing forms when he was two?"

Mr. Lombardi squinted into the sun, cheeks pinking in the wind. "Well, maybe he was older than that," he replied, softly. "And Adam? He loved to build things. Erecting Lincoln Log resorts, LEGO skyscrapers. I'd catch him bossing friends around, delegating responsibility. Like a little foreman." Mr. Lombardi laughed to himself, like he was privately recalling a terrific, precious memory that he'd always hold close to his heart, the kind I was sure to miss out on.

He scowled at me. "There's that look again." He gestured toward Aiden, who squealed as the older boys spun him around. "It's a lovely winter's day. You're here with your son. What could possibly be so bad? You hear all those boys laughing? Have you ever heard such a beautiful sound?"

I pulled my cigarettes, trying to smile. "Just got some bad news, Mr. Lombardi. No big deal."

"*Gerry*," he said, clamping a hand on my shoulder. "Sorry about your bad news. But—" he stabbed a stout finger at Aiden, "*that* little boy there makes it all worthwhile. Don't you forget that!"

"I won't, Mr. Lombardi. I mean, Gerry."

He sighed. "Trouble with the ex?"

I shook the match head. "Sort of."

"It's so hard on these little ones coming from broken homes. See it all the time with UpStart. No matter how much parents love their children, it isn't the same when Mom and Dad aren't together. How old is he again?"

"He'll be two in a couple months."

"That's a *bit* young for UpStart. But in a few years, you might want to think about enrolling him. Getting to at-risk kids early is key. Wait too long, there's the danger of drugs or gangs, or worse."

"Aiden's not 'at risk,'" I said.

"You know, eighty-five percent of the boys in UpStart come from single-parent households. It's true. Statistically, boys who grow up in a single-parent household are almost fifty times more likely to experiment with drugs before they are in high school. Did you know that? Fifty times! And we now know a large component of addiction is genetic." He shifted his gaze to me, touchingly. "How is your brother?"

"Good," I said. "He just opened up a business for himself, in fact." Which was, technically, true.

Mr. Lombardi raised his bristly gray brows. "That's great to hear."

With much effort, he pushed himself back up, smiling over the sea of cavorting boys, before fervently gripping my hand. "You think about what I said." He pointed at Aiden. "When you're ready, you enroll your boy in UpStart. We'll take good care of him."

* * *

I don't think I did as good a job of hiding my stress from Aiden on the way back. I knew Mr. Lombardi had only been trying to help—he was really active in UpStart—but it struck a sour chord. What if Jenny and I already were doing irreparable harm to Aiden, simply by not being together? I didn't think a two-year-old child was in danger of ending up like Chris, but who knows how that works? Lombardi scared the hell out of me. I was a nervous wreck by the time I'd dropped off Aiden at Jenny's.

Brody's truck was gone. Jenny asked if I wanted to come in for coffee and talk. I told her I had to go to work. Then I gave my boy an extralong hug.

I rang Tom and was in the middle of leaving a message, telling him that if anything came up, anything at all, I sure could use the work, when the call cut out. Didn't matter. He'd already told me the score. But I needed to be moving, feeling like I was doing something. In times like these, doing anything is always preferable to doing nothing.

I stared out my fogged-up windshield, panning over the cluster of dumpy efficiencies and converted attic apartments like mine, the spattering of depressing bars and discount retail stores, all crammed into a claustrophobic downtown center. I'd lived here practically my entire life. Even when I went to stay with my aunt and uncle down in Concord after the accident, I was never really gone, taking bus rides back on the weekends until I was old enough to drive myself, calling my best friend Charlie to stay up on the latest. I attended all the Ashton High proms and homecomings. I could never escape Ashton. I had remained tethered to its earth like an old farmer rooted to withering, diminished crops, simply because I couldn't think of anything better to do.

It wasn't yet eleven o'clock. I had no work for the foreseeable future, which meant I finally had the chance to do all the shit I'd been complaining about not having the time to do. Only, I couldn't think of a damned thing.

I didn't feel like going back to my shithole apartment and being alone, watching the same DVDs I'd already seen half a dozen times and drinking beer until it was time for a nap, so I called up Charlie, even though I knew there wasn't a chance in hell he'd be out of bed yet. For

Charlie, Friday nights meant tying one on in order to forget another soul-sucking week working for the phone company. He'd be passed out till three, at least. He didn't pick up. I headed there anyway.

I'd known Charlie since elementary school, and when I'd come back from Concord for the weekends, I'd often stay at his house, which he inherited from his mother after she'd died of cancer his senior year. I didn't understand how he could still live there. Even if the bank hadn't swooped in and snatched our house, I doubted I could've stayed long. It felt weird roaming the same rooms where people you cared about, but who now were gone, had once called your name.

A split-level on over an acre and a half of land, Charlie's place was before the foothills in the low-lying plains that stretched for miles, countryside awash in a sea of white and spired evergreens. His mom's old red Subaru was still parked in front of the garage, tires deflated, shell coated in grime and tree sap. Flowerbeds, long left untended, were now overrun with brush and bramble, buried beneath fallen limbs from the storm.

I rapped on the aluminum frame of the screen door. Doorbell hadn't worked in years. No answer. I pounded with the ball of my fist. When Charlie crashed, he crashed hard.

I knew he was home. His repair van was parked drunkenly beside the grounded riding mower that he'd given up on fixing. Last night he'd asked me to stop by the Dubliner, the pub along East Main where he played in a dart league, the primary social activity in his life. I might've done so had it not been for Chris. Probably not, though. I didn't have much patience for the bar scene any more. I preferred to drink my beer alone, without being subjected to the inane banter of idiots. The girls who went to the Dubliner kept getting younger and easier, which sounds good on the surface, except that I didn't give a damn about singing competitions or vampires, and it got depressing after a while, pretty heads full of rocks.

Even when I'd pick up a girl, winning was still losing. After a regrettable night of pissing away money on some dopey girl I didn't even like, I'd wake up in a hungover fog, having forgotten who was in my bed. When I'd roll over and see that it wasn't Jenny, my heart would break all over again.

"What time is it?" Charlie asked, shielding his eyes from the harsh morning glare.

"Almost eleven."

"Jesus Christ. I was sleeping."

"Try waking at a normal hour."

His head looked like it'd been trampled by the business end of a harvester, deep pillow marks grooved into his puffy face, the kind you get from passing out and remaining in the same position for hours. He whisked me inside and then shut the door, sealing us in musty darkness.

Charlie hadn't redecorated since his mom died, and the house retained that old-lady feel, all décor left over from the 1970s—paisley print sofas and wagon-wheel coffee tables, shitty paintings that you could buy for a quarter at any garage sale up here, because at one time or another every retiree in New Hampshire tries their hand at painting. The spice rack that hung by the sink housed herbs that had to be at least thirty years old. Don't know why he needed spices. Charlie didn't cook.

Charlie scratched his naked, pink belly, which slung over his gray sweats like a jumbo canned ham, before retying the drawstring, as if that would make a difference. He'd started to inherit that classic drunkard's face, where the head seems to swell a bit, pulling back roots at the temple, nose blossoming, complexion permanently rosy, entire visage swollen like a bad allergic reaction. Charlie used to be a good-looking guy, but he was seriously slipping.

Still not fully awake, Charlie dragged his bare feet to the cupboards, swatting aside bags of chips and packages of cookies, other junk foods, searching for the coffee tin. "Where were you last night?"

I sat at the kitchen table and lit a cigarette. "Had to pick up my brother from the police station."

"What'd he do this time?"

"Does it matter?" I rearranged the salt and pepper shakers, fingered the saucer he used for an ashtray. "Jenny and Aiden are moving to Rutland."

"Vermont? When?" Charlie filled a pot under the faucet.

"Soon as Brody finds a house."

Charlie chuckled as he sifted coffee grounds. "I wouldn't sweat it. That dipshit couldn't find his own ass with both hands."

"Supposedly he's got this manager's gig waiting for him down there. Foreman position. Been in the works a while, I think."

"I'll believe it when I see it." Charlie flipped the switch. The rich smells of brewing coffee wafted over the small room. "Either way, you've got plenty of time." He dug out the sugar, spooned some into a bowl. "Can't buy a house overnight. Gotta get a loan. There's a mortgage and pre-approval, realtors, banks, short sales, foreclosures, haggling on a price. It takes a long time, man. Fisher's going through it right now, trying to sell his mother's house."

"Fisher's back?"

"No. Still lives in Concord. Just up here helping with the sale. Taking forever." Charlie leaned against the counter. "If they haven't even started looking yet, could be a year or more."

"But it's going to happen," I said. "Eventually. Even if it's a year or more, it's still going to happen."

"This was your problem back in high school," Charlie said. "You undersell yourself."

"We didn't go to high school together."

"Like you weren't back every weekend. Man, you never left this place." Charlie winked. "But you should've."

"And gone where?"

"You were the smartest guy I knew," Charlie said. "You read actual books, took school serious, got good grades. And you were creative too. Remember that story you wrote? The one about your parents going on vacation and leaving you with your brother, and he locked you under the porch with nothing to eat but spiders?"

"I was goofing around."

"It was funny as hell. You gave me that story up at the reservoir, and in the fall I passed it around to everyone in class. We busted our guts over it. You could've been an author or something. Nobody thought up shit like you did. You had talent. Could've gone to college, somewhere far from here. California or whatever."

"That isn't how it works. You need parents to foot the bill. Or else be able to shoot a ball through a hoop."

"How would you know? You never even took the shot." Charlie wrinkled his nose. "You're sweating a joker like Brody? There are a million guys like Brody." Charlie pointed at me. "There's only one Jay Porter."

The coffee finished percolating, and Charlie filled two mugs. He set them down with the sugar in front of me, then grabbed a carton of milk from the fridge, sniffed it, decided it didn't smell too bad, and joined me at the table. He swiped a cigarette from my pack and perched an elbow over the back of the chair, digging around his craw for whatever he had stuck in his molars.

I dumped in some sugar and milk and stirred.

"We both know why you came back," Charlie said, scratching the thinning curls of his kinky hair. "Why you couldn't leave. I don't have any brothers or sisters, so feel free to tell me I don't know what the fuck I'm talking about."

"You don't know what the fuck you're talking about."

Charlie grinned. "The sooner you cut bait with your brother, the better your life is gonna get. Don't get me wrong. I *like* the guy. He's always been cool with me. He's just, I'm sorry, man, a lost cause, dead weight."

"Last night was the first time I've seen my brother in almost six months," I said.

"Ain't no 'almost.' You know exactly when you seen him last."

It had been five months and thirteen days. But I knew that only because Chris had come by begging for money on his birthday, like junkies are entitled to get high on their birthdays. We'd had this huge fight, which ended with him screaming outside my window, "But it's my *birthday!*"

"I'd rather talk about Jenny right now," I said.

Charlie flashed a quizzical look. "I thought we were."

My cell buzzed on the table. A number I didn't recognize. Normally,

I wouldn't take the call. But given recent developments, I held up a finger and answered.

"I need it back." It was a man's voice, though not a very assured one. He sounded pretty young, in fact.

"Need what back?" I asked.

"I need it back," he repeated, a little more desperately this time.

Charlie eyed me from across the table.

"I think you have the wrong—"

"I dropped off a computer the other day. By mistake. But I want— I *need* to get it back."

"Who is this?"

"Please," the man begged. "I have money. I'll pay you." He sounded as if he was on the verge of tears.

"How'd you get this number?" An incoming call was waiting. "Hold on," I said, and switched over. "Hello?"

"Jay. It's me. Turley."

"Christ, Turley. What do you want now?"

"We have a problem."

"Wrong," I said. "*You* have a problem. I told you, I don't know where this guy Pete is. I'm not doing your job for you."

"Jay, they found Pete Naginis' body behind the Travel Center Truck Stop about an hour ago. His neck's been broken. There's an APB out for your brother."

"Hold on, Turley."

I switched over to the other line. It was dead.

CHAPTER SIX

Three squad cars, about half of Ashton's entire fleet, were parked helter-skelter beside an ambulance with its rear doors flung open at the far end of the Travel Center lot where the semis regularly lined up and rested for the night. Currently, there were half a dozen tractor-trailers stacked up there, nose to bumper, drivers either still asleep in their cabs or else stocking up inside before heading back out on the trail.

The sprawling facility had every accessory and accommodation for a trucker's needs. Showers, laundry machines. There was a convenience store and a restaurant, the Peachtree, with the Maple Motor Inn a skip away, in case a driver needed more room to stretch out or whatever.

We parked my Chevy in front the Peachtree. We couldn't get much closer, what with the crime scene tape and gaggle of onlookers that had assembled. Walking toward the scene, Charlie, who'd insisted on coming along, cinched the furred hood of his parka tighter, as I tried to fathom what this would mean for my brother.

The TC was right off the Turnpike, a busy thoroughfare for deliveries from southern New England up to Canada. It actually was a straighter shot than the I-93, and frequently less congested, making it the preferred route for many long-haul drivers. The Turnpike was barely within Ashton's city limits, just clipping its northeastern tip. Given the TC's scandalous reputation, there had been periodic squawking about shutting it down. But since so many local factories and mills had gone under in recent years, the Travel Center provided one of the few consistent revenue streams for the town, and so any chatter of closing it eventually died off. Most chose to ignore its existence. Out of sight, out of mind. The TC was Ashton's dirty secret, a small town's red-light district. Which was fine, as long as the riffraff remained out of sight. Who really gave a shit about a trucker getting a blow job from a toothless junkie? Live free or die, man. But a murder, even of a scumbag drug addict, was bound to incite an uproar.

Plowed snow clustered around lampposts, towering twelve, fifteen feet high, like mammoth mounds of mashed potatoes. Earsplitting noise assaulted on all fronts as traffic flew past on the Turnpike, and countless industrial-sized laundry and dishwashing machines whirred and buzzed.

Through the glut of cops, EMTs, reporters, and gawking rubberneckers, I spotted Sheriff Pat Sumner standing in the middle of the crime scene. A little old man, he'd been sheriff up here since before I was born. He tapped Turley, who turned and made his way toward us, pushing through the fracas, gleefully waving a hand over his head.

"Charlie Finn," Turley called out with a big goofy grin, like a nerd trying to sniff himself into a jock's good graces. "Been a while. Where you been hiding?"

Charlie thumbed over his shoulder. "I live five miles down the road. Same house I grew up in."

Turley's face pinched and he squinched one eye, scratching his furry, Chia Pet head. "How come I never see you?"

"I don't know, Turley. Have you been looking?"

"Good point, Charlie," Turley said with a laugh. "Good point."

"What's up?" I said.

"Not good, Jay." Turley turned sideways, pointing to a line of skinny, bare birches at the back end of a blue brick building that was tagged with graffiti and cordoned off with yellow police tape. "Waitress went out for a smoke, found the body in the wastewater runoff. Ligature marks—that means he was strangled—face bashed in pretty good. Neck been broke."

"So, why are you looking for my brother?"

Even Charlie seemed taken aback by my question. I recognized how ridiculous it sounded. Of course they'd be looking for him. But I also knew that Chris couldn't have done this in a million years.

"Um," Turley stammered. "Just need to talk to him, is all."

"I don't know where he is."

Eighteen wheels rumbled over the snow-packed asphalt, an endless parade of trucks downshifting, chugging, rumbling bellies of braking semis belching diesel fumes into the lot. Hard gusts raced over the peaks of Lamentation Mountain, swooping down brae to brow. Whipping through tightly crowded, manmade spaces, flecks of snow and tiny ice chips kicked up and stung exposed skin. I blew on my hands, red and raw.

"You need to try to find him," Turley said. "There's a lot of pressure coming from on high."

"On high?" repeated Charlie. "What are you talking about? You got a police force of what, half a dozen?"

"That's the thing," Turley said, inching closer, peering back at a man in a suit.

Crisp overcoat, leather gloves, glistening shoes. The man stood talking to Sheriff Sumner and a deputy, Ollie Gibson, scribbling something down. It's funny, when you spend your whole life in a small town, people who don't belong stand out like ten-foot aliens belting show tunes.

"Came up from the city," Turley said. "Detective."

"Why is a Concord detective up here investigating a dead junkie behind a truck stop?" I asked.

Turley shrugged.

The detective briefly glanced my way. Aromas from the crappy fried food they served in the Peachtree drifted over, mixing with the cigarette smoke and diesel emissions; it smelled nauseous.

I gestured toward the detective, who'd already returned to jotting notes. "Is he going to want to talk to me?"

"Eventually, I guess," Turley said. He looked me squarely in the eyes. "I'm granting you a courtesy."

"A courtesy?"

"Yeah," Turley said, testily. "A courtesy. A favor. Now do *yourself* a favor. Find Chris. Get him to come down on his own so we can straighten this out. I don't know why they sent a detective all the way from Concord. But you're right. It's weird. The drug shit must really be getting folks riled up. Last thing Michael Lombardi's campaign needs is a drug-related murder in his hometown." Anticipating what I was about to say next, Turley quickly added, "No one is saying Chris is guilty of anything. But Naginis *was* killed. And your brother was heard making threats. It's hardly a leap." Turley looked me dead on. "I know what you think of me, Jay. I'm not stupid. But I'm doing you a solid here. I hope you see that." He thumbed back at the scene and the Concord detective. "That guy isn't messing around. He's treating this like a big deal investigation. I don't think you want us finding your brother first."

***

"That was fucking weird," Charlie said as we pulled away from the TC.

I fiddled with the knob, trying to dial in some music, news, sports, car talk—anything to put noise between my racing thoughts and the ramifications. Nothing but static, frequencies jammed, signals lost almost immediately.

"What did he mean by that last part?" Charlie asked. "'You don't want us finding him first'—what the hell?"

"Turley's watched too many cop shows, I think."

Charlie chuckled, but it wasn't funny, and neither of us thought Turley had been blowing smoke. I considered Turley a self-aggrandizing jackass when it came to most things law enforcement, but this was for real. As much as I wanted to dismiss his warning as chest puffing, I couldn't. Chris had really fucked up this time. I knew my brother didn't kill Pete; he didn't have that kind of violence in him. But what he *could* do was to seriously make a mess of things. He'd made a career of it. And this was a perfect shit-storm: the wrong thing said at the wrong time, heard by the wrong person, and aided by the worst possible circumstances. My brother had threatened to kill a dead man. I needed to find him before I was powerless to help him.

Ashton may not have been New York City, but the town was hardly a stranger to violence, especially at that truck stop. A couple summers back, a prostitute had been found badly beaten and left in a dumpster. But there'd never been a detective up from Concord to investigate before. This was bigger than some run-of-the-mill lowlife fished out of a river.

I hadn't mentioned the strange phone call to Turley. Charlie had obviously been listening. We'd talked about it and Chris' visit on our way to the TC. Last night, I'd believed the computer story was another one of my brother's myriad delusions—Chris suffered fits of paranoia like some people get heartburn after eating spicy food—but following that bizarre phone call and the discovery of Pete's body, I knew his conspiracy theories weren't going to be so easy to write off this time.

If the cops were looking for Chris, that computer shop of his would be the first place they'd check out. But dope fiends and crackheads aren't going to be as forthright with the police as they might be with someone else. I offered to drop Charlie home first. He insisted on coming along. Fine by me. I didn't want to deal with this freak show all on my own.

* * *

Turley was right, I knew the spot. Taking the old Pearl Street exit off the Desmond Turnpike, we dipped into a heavily forested gully, and the surrounding scenery began to take on a vaguely familiar appearance, like the edges of a repressed, unpleasant dream. When a dilapidated red shack came into view, I clearly recalled driving by the place on the way to Coal Creek. Never ate the food, though. Even back then, you'd have to have had a death wish to go in there.

It always had been an odd location for a restaurant, since there were few other stores in the vicinity, and you'd have to be literally wandering, starving in the woods to stumble upon it. You could barely see it from the road with all the overgrowth around it.

As we pulled in the small parking lot, a big man with a shaved head, slathered with tattoos and dressed in only a tank top, flicked his cigarette butt in the snow and ducked inside. As the door closed he caught it with his hand and eyed my truck, before gently easing it shut.

The shack projected that creepy-crawly, frenetic energy of amphetamine abuse and long nights spent picking at invisible bugs. Grinding, industrial music droned inside. I could see single tire tracks, like the kind a motorcycle leaves, etched through high snow, curling around back. Long slivers of faded red wood curled from the exterior like whittled plastic.

In a particularly depressing touch, someone had actually taken the time to set out a sandwich board, using portable letters to spell "Computer Solutions," and, below that, "Electronic Recycling." Only, instead of the letter *t*, they had substituted the number *7*, and the word "Recycling" was missing the *y*.

The entire setup played like a rabid, ugly porcupine, whose quills and foaming mouth said, in no uncertain terms, stay away.

Charlie and I sat in the parking lot. I didn't know what I had been expecting. Certainly not this.

"What the fuck is your brother into?"

I knew a little about the local drug scene, only because I had to, but I didn't know what these people did behind closed doors, and I wasn't itching to find out.

Chris would inject, inhale, or imbibe anything you put on the table, although he seemed to have a special affinity for uppers, primarily speed, one of the many sordid particulars I had gathered from all the times I'd brought him into rehab, stuck as I was playing the parental role. Talking to doctors and psychotherapists about my brother's various treatment options, I learned that methamphetamine wasn't mass-produced up here or controlled by organized crime like it was out West or in the South. Meth up here consisted mostly of the bathtub variety. Small, independent pockets of ambitious individuals who cooked batches in toolsheds or suburban basements, crushing antihistamines to strip pseudoephedrine from over-the-counter cold medicines, before cleaning it with acetone and plopping copper pennies into stainless steel bowls to reverse polarity, in order to bond the right ionic charge. Like a science project for sleep-deprived zombies. Gun bluing and industrial-strength ammonia, miner's coal and jet fuel, corrosive chemicals you find under a sink. Basically, the very last kind of ingredients you want to put in your body, and this had been my brother's primary diet for years. No wonder his brain was oozing out his ears. In a few years, he'd be draped in garbage bags and talking to beer cans at the bus station.

I stared at this shooting gallery, this crack den, this drug house, this whatever the hell it was in the middle of nowhere, and steeled my nerves to open my eyes to a part of my brother's life I would've preferred not to have seen. For years, I'd put up a hand over my face and blocked these views from sight. Now I had no choice but to peel back the blinders, willingly step inside, and have a good look around.

"What are you going to do?" Charlie asked. "Just knock on the door?"

"I don't suggest sitting here," I said. Another thing I knew about speed: that shit made you jumpy. "Liable to get a shotgun stuck in our faces."

"I figured we were going to be dropping in on some druggies playing video games," Charlie said. "This place ain't right." He swallowed hard.

I made for my door handle. "You can wait here, if you want."

My work boots crunched snowy stone. I kept my hands out of my pockets. A moment later, I heard Charlie's door slam behind me.

As we drew nearer, the music churned louder, grating and dissonant.

The door was ajar. I slowly pushed it open.

There was scarcely any light, just whatever natural gray filtered through the windows. It took a moment for my eyes to adjust. When they did, I found the big, bald-headed man with the tattoos and wife-beater waiting. He didn't look happy to see us.

It was as cold inside as it was out, not even a space heater, but he didn't wear a jacket, just the tank top, the word "Bowman" stretched across his broad chest in cracked vinyl letters. He had shoulders the size of bowling balls and the Star of David etched into his neck.

Behind him, three other men with the kind of inked-up bodies you get only from long stints in prison, matching flaming-wing-and-gun tattoos, glanced up from a card table where they sat. Workers on an assembly line, screwdrivers and solder in hand, huddled over a mound of squiggling computer innards. Tendrils of smoke slithered from ashtrays and melting wires. You could taste the chemicals burning. But it was what was beyond them that really caught my attention.

On the grimy floor, a half dozen malnourished girls and boys lay, their gangly arms and legs intertwined, blissed-out heads resting in each other's laps or drooping in a nod. The girls appeared woefully underage and whorishly dressed, the boys all weak and thin. It was easy to see my brother was not among them.

The inside of the shop was gutted like a construction site. Sheet-rock had been kicked in, exposing two-by-fours, bands of electrical wires yanked out and dangling, the concrete floor covered in crumbly plaster and nails. The shrill metal music wrenched to an out-of-time beat.

The junkies lazily stirred, like cold-blooded lizards unable to re-animate for lack of sun, pawing, groping, grasping. They looked barely alive, fighting to keep their eyes open. I felt disdain for the whole sorry lot well inside me. Who chooses to live like this?

Then I saw the bruises. Up and down arms, around the wrists, deep blues and purples. My eyes darted to a dark corner and a wood chair. No one sat in it, but twine hung loose from the arms and legs. Liquid pooled underneath, as if someone had pissed himself.

"Can I help you?" Bowman said. It wasn't really a question.

I'd been in a few bar fights over the years, and I had some weight on me, but at that moment I was really glad Charlie had agreed to come along. I was out of my element here.

"I'm looking for my brother," I said, unable to think of anything better.

Maybe the honesty disarmed him, or maybe that was the whole sizing-up process and I didn't pose a threat—I don't know—but Bow-man eased up, haunches and shoulders relaxing. He sniffed hard, grabbed his pack of Camels off what used to be the hostess station, struck a match, and took a long pull, tip glowing cherry red. He blew a ring of smoke in my direction.

"Who's your brother?"

"Chris Porter," I said. "I thought this was his computer shop?"

Bowman peered over his shoulder. The men at the table chuckled.

"He ain't been around here lately," Bowman said, before affecting the mannerisms of the world's most unconvincing receptionist. "But if he stops in, who should I say was asking?"

Charlie and I looked at each other.

The guys behind Bowman laughed some more.

Then he turned to the boom box, a monstrosity from the '80s, cranking the shrill noise louder, and went back to talking to his boys like we weren't even there.

"Did you know Pete?" Charlie shouted above the grind. "Pete Naginis?"

I elbowed Charlie to shut up.

"Because the cops just found his body," Charlie said, "over by the truck stop."

That caught Bowman's attention. He spun and stepped to Charlie, hard.

"The fuck, you say?"

"Nothing," said Charlie, backing up.

"He means the police called to tell me one of my brother's friends had died," I said, wedging in front of Charlie. "They're looking for my brother. It's better if I'm the one to tell him."

Bowman smirked. "Better for who?"

* * *

Trace flurries drifted from a silver sky, wipers swishing in a lullaby. Fast cars whisked past us going in the opposite direction, as the sounds of spinning wet tires on pavement echoed down the valley boulevard, lost to the menacing tower of Lamentation Mountain.

As we drove back to his place, Charlie and I didn't speak. You grow up in a small town like ours and you develop a false sense of security; you forget that beyond county lines lurk predators much bigger than you. Bigger. Tougher. Meaner. And a helluva lot more dangerous.

"What are you going to do?" Charlie asked as I pulled up his driveway.

"I don't know. Wait for my brother to call. Hope he does before the cops pick him up. Or maybe those guys at the shop will tell him I was looking for him." I wanted to add, "if they don't break his neck first," but I was pretty sure that was implied.

"You going to call Turley? Y'know, about what we saw?"

"What did we see, Charlie? Nothing. A bunch of drug addicts and biker dudes."

"What about the chair?"

"A chair with some rope? What do I say? There's a bunch of junkies lying on the floor who aren't looking so good? I told those guys my name. What's going to happen when the cops show up half an hour after we left?"

I lit a cigarette and gazed over his yard, which connected to an old farm, which connected to another old farm and another old farm, until the mountain range rose up to define our borders, like the glass walls of a snow globe. That's what it felt like too. As if some prankster god had scooped up my world and given it a hearty shake, and now was sitting back, laughing.

"I want to find my brother," I said. "But going up there was a mistake. This really has nothing to do with me."

"You remember I was telling you about Fisher?"

"What about him?"

"He's an investigator now."

"Fisher's a cop?"

"No. Like, for a private company. I'm not sure, exactly, but he's definitely an investigator. He stopped in the Dubliner for a drink a couple weeks back. I was pretty hammered. Maybe he can do something."

"Like what?"

"I don't know," Charlie said, exiting. "But I'll give him a ring. Can't hurt, right?"

I didn't bother to mention that I hadn't talked to Fisher in years, or that the last time I had, I vividly recalled the dude hated my guts. I could hardly refuse the offer.

Our trip to that shop had made one thing abundantly clear: my brother had sunk too deep into the muck this time for me to go wading in to pull out his ass on my own.

CHAPTER SEVEN

Next day, the murder was all over the front page of the *Herald*. The paper didn't speculate on motive, nor did it delve too much into specifics beyond what Turley had already told me. The article didn't come right out and say my brother was a suspect, only that he was wanted for questioning. Pretty much the same thing. The piece mostly broached hot-button peripherals like prostitution and dealing drugs at the TC, with several quotes from town officials proselytizing what needed to be done to eradicate the problems, including an impassioned plea from Adam Lombardi, who said he "hoped this senseless killing would be the wake-up call Ashton needed" to close down the truck stop, which he called "a bad influence and an eyesore." Which was the response you'd expect. It was no secret what took place at the truck stop, but that didn't mean folks wanted it shoved in their faces, either.

I fielded phone calls and questions for the rest of the morning and on through the afternoon. Turley bugged me a couple times. Charlie rang to see how I was holding up. Word had even drifted down to my aunt and uncle in Concord. Though they'd distanced themselves from Chris a while ago, they were still concerned. The only person I wanted to talk to was Jenny, but it was never her on the line, and I was still too angry and prideful to call her. When I went to the market around lunchtime to stock up on beer, I felt everyone staring at me, probably due to my own paranoia. I was anxious to get back to my place and hole up, which made me feel like a prisoner. Finally, I powered down my cell, took the landline off the hook, pulled the blinds, dragged a six-pack to the couch, and cracked open a cold one. I glugged it down. Then I cracked another.

* * *

Ashton wasn't some hick town. We had two supermarkets, a movie theater showing up to three new releases at a time, four pizza and grinder shops, a McDonald's and an Arby's, two banks, a credit union, a barber, a stylist, two dentists, and a Dairy Queen that closed every fall. Plus several liquor stores. Even a football field for the high school. But Ashton was still small enough that everybody knew everybody's business, which made life a lot rougher when you had a brother like mine.

I was eight years old when my parents died. I should've had more than enough time to put the loss behind me. Only I hadn't. The tragedy was woven into my very person, like cigarette smoke on a cable-knit after a long night at the bar. I couldn't put the accident behind me because small-town innuendo wouldn't let me, and I knew this latest fiasco with Chris would only grease the rumor mill wheels. Turley wasn't the only one. Everyone had heard that goddamn story, and even when people didn't bring it up, you could still tell they were thinking it, which made it just as bad. Sometimes what *isn't* said can be every bit as damning as what *is*.

For a while, it was just Chris and I living in the house. He had a good job at Hank Miller's garage. Chris was a pro when it came to fixing cars. Wasn't a motor he couldn't put back together blindfolded. He'd had a shot to attend college on a wrestling scholarship, but he stuck around. He stuck around, in part, to help take care of me, which is something you don't forget, no matter how bad someone turns out.

That Chris and our father had fought so much publicly didn't help the situation. They were always at each other's throats. Once, at a wrestling meet, they had to be physically separated. Another time, they got into a shoving match in the DQ parking lot. Chris was messing with drugs even then. Mostly pot, I think. Hash. Acid. I hated being in the middle of it. Like our mom, I steered clear and tried not to pick sides. Maybe I was a coward. What did I really know? Like the drowning story, I couldn't trust my own memories. Chris never wanted to talk about it, except to call the old man an asshole, and there was no point poking that dog now. We were way past the talking stage.

All kinds of shit happens when your parents die and you're still a kid—executors, creditors, social services, mortgages and banks, court orders, insurance claims—a bureaucratic nightmare that neither Chris nor I had been equipped to handle, not that it should've been my responsibility at all.

I didn't blame my brother. He'd done his best. He was just a kid out of high school, and he'd always been off somewhat, head screwy, easily rattled. Chris began drinking more, getting high more, fighting with everyone. Honestly, it was almost a relief when the bank finally tacked up that notice. When my Aunt Dee Dee brought me down to Concord, I worried about leaving Chris behind.

They never talked about Chris living with us in Concord. The police had spoken with Dee Dee plenty, and already people were regarding my brother as a lost cause. I doubt Chris would've accepted an offer anyway. Dee Dee was our father's sister and the spitting image of him, and Chris hated her too. Chris still had his job, girlfriends; he got an apartment in town. He liked living in Ashton. How could I know he'd end up on the street?

Every time I came back, he seemed further gone. I worried about him constantly, which made it hard to concentrate on my future. I'd always been good at school, got straight As, just came naturally, didn't need to study much or anything. Guidance counselors and my aunt pushed me to apply to colleges. I even flew to check out a couple. In the end, though, I felt I needed to get home.

When I moved back after graduation and saw how bad Chris had gotten, I did everything I could to make it right. I could still talk to him then, and I thought I could fix him. I'd convince him to try and sober up. I'd drag him into detox units, plead with rehab counselors, begging them to help him. They'd calmly explain that you can't help someone who isn't willing to help himself. I'd get so angry, screaming, accusing them of callousness and not doing their jobs. Of course, they were right.

* * *

I woke in a cold, dark place, empty cans and plastic rings littering my lap, head clogged like I'd just landed after a long, turbulent flight and had forgotten the chewing gum. I thumbed on my cell. 10:41. A few lousy beers shouldn't have been able to knock me out like that. Probably the stress. These last couple days hadn't been easy.

Stumbling to the bathroom, I set the landline on the hook. A second later it rang.

"What the hell?" Charlie said. "I've been calling for two hours. Who you been talking to this long?"

"Nobody."

"Listen, what are you doing right now?"

"Going to sleep." From the background chatter, I could tell he was calling me from the bar. I knew he was going to try and drag me down there.

"Any luck finding your brother?"

"No." I dug my cigarettes from my jeans pocket. My nameless cat rubbed against my leg. I took a drag. "Honestly, he could be dead in a ditch like Pete. Wouldn't even know it."

"Come down to the Dubliner, meet me for a drink."

My head throbbed. My bones ached. The biting north winds swirled outside, rattling the windowpanes. No way was I going out in that cold.

"Not tonight, man."

"What?" Charlie scoffed. "You got something better to do?"

"It's late. It's been a long day. I need to get some sleep."

"C'mon, one beer," Charlie pleaded. "I've been working on how to solve your problem."

"What problem?"

He paused for an exaggerated moment. "Chris! What do you think I'm talking about?"

"I don't know, Charlie, you called me."

I thought I heard someone outside my door.

"For me? Please? Just one beer. You'll be glad you did. Promise."

Someone rapped lightly. Then tried the handle.

"Okay," I said under my breath. "Half an hour." I quickly hung up.

The handle jiggled harder this time.

I hadn't turned on the lights in the apartment, the room blacked out, but I could see shadows moving beneath the front door gap from the bulb that blazed all night in the stairwell. I walked softly across the floor, peering out the living room window into the street. Through the halo of streetlamp and drifting snow, I didn't see any recently parked cars; each one was covered with a good few inches of fresh powder.

Who the hell would visit this time of night? Without calling first? I didn't believe my brother would risk coming here, not with everyone on his ass. Hank Miller lived in the house next door, but he never stopped by without a heads up. One of the reasons I kept renting from the guy; he respected my privacy. Then I remembered those junkie bikers from the shop.

"Open up. I know you're home," Jenny said, voice muffled behind the door. "I can hear you tiptoeing around in there."

Christ, I was acting as fidgety as my brother.

"What are you doing here?" I asked, flicking on the lights and opening the door.

"That's a nice way to greet someone," Jenny said as she slipped past. She was bundled up head to toe, like a little kid with an overprotective mom on a snow day, button nose wind-nipped and pink. "I wouldn't have to come out in the freezing cold if you'd answer your phone."

"Where's Aiden?"

"At my mom's."

"You scared me," I said. "I thought something was wrong."

"No, our son is fine. A terror. But fine." She smiled weakly. "He dropped Brody's keys in the toilet today. And then flushed." She waited for me to say something. "Don't worry," she said. "We were able to fish them out."

"Glad to hear it."

She furiously rubbed her hands together. "It's an icebox in here. Is the heat even on?"

"Sorry," I said, and reached behind her and cranked up the radiator. The old pipes sputtered and coughed like an old man with a chest infection. "Gas bills, y'know?"

"If you need to take back some of that money, Jay—"

"I'm good."

I kicked out a chair for her. Only had the one. Leg had broken on the other, and even though I worked with used furniture practically every day, I hadn't gotten around to replacing it. Wasn't exactly hosting a lot of dinner parties.

"Have a seat," I said. "To what do I owe the pleasure?" Which was a ridiculous thing to say, and her face screwed up, letting me know it. I didn't understand how she could still make me so nervous after all we'd been through together. It was like, whenever I got around her, I instantly reverted to a fourth grade dweeb, stomach knotted, scared to hold hands on the jungle gym because my palms might get sweaty. It also made me defensive, which could make me sound like a dick. Plus, I was still pissed off about the move. I wasn't going to bring it up first and give her the satisfaction. I'd just wait for an opening when it would do the most damage. I knew I should be bigger than that. But I wasn't going to be.

"Can't I stop by and say hello?" she asked, peeling back the hood of her parka. For a moment, the way her long, brown hair fell so softly, her playful smile etched on pretty lips, it made me forget how angry I was at her for taking my son to Rutland with that dillweed hillbilly. In that instant, she was just that girl I had fallen in love with all those years ago, drinking beer on the banks of Coal Creek as the summer slipped away and we dreamt big.

"I read about your brother," she said. "How are you doing?"

I went to the fridge, grabbed a beer. I held it up behind my back.

"No thanks," Jenny said.

"Suit yourself." I cracked it open and took a hearty slug, then wiped my mouth with the back of my sleeve and belched. It was the most bachelor thing I could think to do.

"What are your plans?" she asked.

"For what?"

I started gathering dishes shellacked with food scraps and empty to-go containers off the table, dropping crusted pots and stained coffee mugs in the sink, soaping hot water to let them soak. The place was a pigsty. It stank. I hadn't done laundry in a month. I balled soiled tees and chucked them in the corner. Then dragged the trashcan from under the sink and started dumping ashtrays and plastic lids overflowing with cigarette butts.

Jenny crossed over and took my hands in hers. "What are you doing?"

"What's it look like? Cleaning up my apartment. You should be happy. You're always bitching about what a slob I am."

She stared empathetically. "Talk to me."

"There's nothing to talk about."

"You must be worried about your brother."

"What do you care? It's not your problem anymore."

"Don't be stupid. I still care what happens to you."

"You do?"

"Of course I do, Jay."

I broke from her grip. "But that's not stopping you from moving five hours away, is it?"

"That's not fair."

"Not fair? You mean, like not discussing moving with my son to another state? Like buying a house with some rebound fuck. Like not giving me a chance—"

"A chance? I've given you nothing *but* chances. To spend more time with Aiden. To catch up on payments. To fix us. And what have you done? Nothing. Absolutely nothing."

"I just gave you money."

"It's not about money."

"What's it about then?"

"Your priorities, Jay. How you chose to focus your energy and spend your time. It's about you not settling for less when you're worth so much more."

"I know you think you're paying me some twisted compliment when you say stuff like that, like you're building up my self-worth or something. But you're not. All I hear is that I'm not good enough."

"Then you're mishearing me—because that is *not* what I am saying."

"This is a really rotten time to be laying this on me. I'm in the middle of this shit with my brother."

"What do you think I'm talking about?"

"Here it comes."

"Here *what* comes?"

"You hate my brother. You've always hated him."

"No, I don't."

"Bullshit."

Jenny stepped back, arms akimbo. "That's where you're wrong. I don't hate Chris. I actually like your brother. When he's not all fucked up. I think he's sick, and I feel sorry for him. I see how hard it is on you. I think he needs help. But you can't be the one to fix him."

"I gave up trying to fix him a long time ago. But I'm not abandoning him, either."

"No one is asking you to. You have to find a way to distance yourself, though. You can't keep making *his* habit *your* problem. Whatever he's done this time—"

"He didn't *do* anything," I said, "other than be his usual screw-up self. Wrong place. Wrong time."

"Then let him answer for himself. You can't shoulder that stone."

"What do you suggest I do?"

"Let Chris deal with Chris' mess."

"Nice, Jenny. When they fish him out of a dumpster behind the truck stop, I hope you feel good."

"No, I won't feel good," she said. "But I won't feel guilty, either."

"He's family."

She stared at me, urgently. "You keep saying that. Don't you see? We're your family too. And you shut us out."

"My family? And what are you doing with *my* family, huh? Packing up and running off with that shitheel to Vermont. You know damn well I'll never get down there. I have a hard enough time making it five miles down the road as it is."

"And whose fault is that?"

"I work, Jenny. I don't have some cushy union job with four weeks' paid vacation. I have to cull a million different projects together, hustle and bust my balls to cobble a halfway decent payday just to keep creditors off my ass. My schedule is irregular; I never know when the work is going to dry up. I need to take advantage of it when I can get it. That means long hours, that means I don't always get weekends off."

"That's your choice. You could do anything you want. You're a bright guy—"

"Gee, thanks."

"—who plays dumb. You sell yourself short, hauling junk for Tom Gable."

"I don't haul junk. And Tom's been good to me."

"I'm sure he has. I like Tom. He's a nice guy. But you could be doing so much more—you still *can* do so much more."

"I'm glad you are such an authority on my life. And I do appreciate the unsolicited advice, really."

"I think you're scared."

"Scared?" I had to laugh. "And what am I scared of?"

"Not being as good a father as your dad. You blame yourself for not being able to fix your brother, and you feel you're letting down his memory. So you deliberately sell yourself short and don't live up to your potential. You suffer. Like a penance."

"Congratulations," I said, jeering. "That's officially the dumbest thing anyone has ever said to me."

"How long do you expect us to wait for you to get your shit together?"

I moved toward her.

"What if I did?" I said.

"What if you did what?" Her eyes blazed with fury as she balled her hands into tiny fists, mouth compressed into a hard, thin line, which is what happened every time I got her worked up, something I possessed an uncanny ability to do.

I stepped closer, and she stuttered a half step back.

"What if I had my shit together?" I said. "What if I had a regular job, a steady paycheck with security and benefits—what if I worked at the phone company like Charlie—punched a clock every morning, came home every night?"

"What if you did?"

I moved in. She backpedaled, bumping against the kitchen table, hands fumbling to grip an edge.

"Would you still be with me?"

She couldn't retreat any farther; I was pressed against her now. She turned her head away. But I had her pinned, my mouth inches from her face as she squirmed half-heartedly.

"I'm not answering that," she said. "It's a stupid question."

"What's so stupid about it?"

Jenny stopped squirming, squared her face to mine. Her hands went to my hips, pulling me in, pressing hard against my jeans. She stared into my eyes.

"Because I never would've left in the first place."

I jerked a hand over her head and snagged my heavy wool coat off the kitchen table. "I have to go."

I left her standing there.

"Thanks for the visit," I said, walking out. "Lock up when you leave."

"You should know, people are saying he killed that guy."

"People are wrong."

I bulled out the door and down those old rickety steps, out into the biting northern winds that felt like a million razors slicing my skin.

CHAPTER EIGHT

The Dubliner was dead, typical for a Sunday night. A few college-aged stragglers looking too preppy for White Mountain Community—but too far from Dartmouth to be Ivy League—played a game of ham-fisted darts in the corner, in between loud sports talk and rape jokes. A pair of white-haired, leather-faces slumped over amber shot glasses along the bar, droopy eyes, poor posture, trying to tuck a lifetime of regret deep down inside and keep it hidden from the light.

On weekends the place could pick up when Liam, the bar's owner, featured his Celtic folk trio, The January Men. The music sucked, but if you cozied up to him afterwards, telling him how great they were, you'd get drinks on the house all night long. Even on Fridays and Saturdays, patrons were mostly locals; nobody would come to a place like the Dubliner unless he lived within a six-block radius.

I didn't see Charlie so I poked my head out on the smoking porch, where I found him—and Fisher—leaning against the long tiki hut counter, island straw and bamboo entirely out of place in an Irish-themed bar in the dead of winter in the Northern wilds. Charlie waved at me; Fisher nodded glumly. The two of them were smoking cigarettes, a pitcher of beer and a basket of chicken wings between them. The cold night air hurt to breathe in.

I'd give Charlie hell later. I knew he'd planned on calling Fisher, but didn't realize he already had, and that that was the urgency behind meeting for a drink. I could've used prep time before having to deal with the guy.

All the umbrellas were strapped down, chairs upended and set atop tables. Deep snow covered the patio floor, except where Charlie and

Fisher stood, a puddle of slush from smokers' trampling. On the walls, a fenced enclosure, hundreds of license plates and other tin sign oddities hung, quirky symbols of Americana from places like Route 66, the Grand Canyon, Amish Country. I remembered being so drunk with Charlie one night that we tried to pry off a chicken ranch sign with a screwdriver.

I'd been gnashing my teeth the whole drive over here. Seeing Fisher only agitated me more. I would've gone back to my place, except I'd left Jenny there, and she was what I wanted to get away from. No one could make me as happy as she could, and no one could piss me off as much.

I was in a helluva mood, and the oily stench of bar food and cloyingly sweet smell of cheap aftershave wasn't helping.

"Hey, man!" Charlie said, perking up too enthusiastically.

Charlie knew Fisher and I didn't get along, which thrust him into the role of peacekeeper whenever we got together. Which didn't happen often. I probably hadn't seen Fisher in three, four years, not since Charlie had pulled the same stunt at an Applebee's in Clear Lake. I think Charlie, who didn't have a lot of friends, secretly held out hope we'd suddenly start liking each other.

Fisher gnawed on BBQ, slurping bits of meat from bone, face and fingers stained muddy red. He waggled a wing at me before flinging it into the cast-off pile.

"So, Porter," he said, "still the king of Shit County?" He snorted. Fisher had packed on some pounds since I'd seen him last. His hair was thinning, but he still wore it longish, in a mullet. Slick, black ringlets curled behind a pair of Dumbo ears. With his bulbous nose and soft chin, Fisher hadn't exactly grown into his looks.

Snow started to fall. Nobody made for the door. I fired up a cigarette and let Charlie pour me the last of the beer.

"Why'd you drag me down here, Charlie?"

Charlie clasped a hand on Fisher's back. "I told you. Fisher's an investigator. He's offered to help us out. Isn't that great?"

"Yeah. Great."

"Why not?" Fisher said, sucking on the bone. "We're all friends here."

His contemptuous tone made it clear he still hated my guts. Our rivalry began at the reservoir one summer, when I felt up Gina Rosinski in the backseat of Sal Atkinson's Buick. Fisher had a thing for Gina, which I only became aware of after the fact. Hell, it was high school. He never got over it. I seriously doubted he was itching to do me any favors.

"I appreciate the offer," I said, "But I don't have money to hire an investigator. I'm sort of out of work right now. I don't know when it's going to pick back up."

Fisher sifted through the basket of wings, searching for a juicy one. "I don't want your money, Porter," he said, as if the mere suggestion was offensive. "Charlie tells me you're in a tight spot. I'm here helping my mom pack up the house—you know she's moving to Florida, right?"

I hadn't seen Fisher's mother in probably fifteen years. How the hell would I know that? I nodded anyway.

"Charlie says you had a run-in with some tough druggie bikers."

"It wasn't exactly a run-in."

"The Desmond Turnpike is a pipeline for dope smuggling," Fisher said. "Boston to Montreal, up, down, all through the night. Better than the I-93." Fisher poked around the discarded bones for any fleshy tidbits he might have missed. "They have video cameras set up all along the Interstate. Highway Patrol records license plates. Same vehicle makes the trip too many times—say 'cheese'! Boom, they pull your ass over. Trust me, I deal with this shit every day."

"So what," I said, "you're, like, a private investigator now?"

"Not private, but, yeah, I'm an investigator." Fisher drained his pint, clinking the bottom of the glass against the counter.

Charlie playfully punched my shoulder, grinning. "See? Aren't you glad I brought you down here? He's offering to help, Jay. And he ain't charging us anything. We could use a pro."

"No, man," Fisher said, "like I say, I'm stuck in this shitburg. You two might like fixing phones—or whatever the hell it is *you* do, Porter, selling lamps at flea markets or some shit—but I got nothing to do during the day. I'm bored out of my mind. Might as well help out a couple old pals, right?"

The barmaid, Rita, Liam's wife, stuck her head out the back door, and Fisher hoisted his empty pint glass and pointed at the empty pitcher.

"If you're not private," I said, "then you work for the police or something?"

"Something like that," Fisher said.

"Something like what?"

"Insurance."

"Insurance?"

"Yeah, insurance," Fisher said, heated. "I investigate fraudulent claims. I do surveillance, videotape assholes trying to steal my company's money with their bullshit scams. I follow them. Use public records. The Internet, eyewitness testimony. Study accident scenes, examine a claimant's past for any recurring patterns of negligence or deception. Conduct interviews, follow up leads, write reports. A fucking investigator. You got a problem with that?" He threw up his hands at Charlie, who motioned with both of his to stay calm.

"He's just worked up about his brother," said Charlie, turning my way. "Right, Jay?"

I nodded. I didn't need any more drama in my life right now.

"Jay, tell him about the hard drive," said Charlie. "That's the key to this whole thing."

Fisher whipped out a tiny notepad and pencil, crinkling his brow as though commencing an exclusive interview.

"Not much to tell," I said. "According to Turley, my brother made some threats, so the cops called me down. Chris and his buddy, Pete—"

"The guy who was killed," Charlie interjected.

"Yeah, the guy who was killed," I said. "They have a business recycling old computers, erasing their memory. Chris claims someone dropped off a computer, and they found something incriminating."

"He say what?"

I shook my head. "He wasn't making much sense. When I picked him up and we went back to my place, he asked if I could keep a secret. But he was also making up stories from when we were kids and quoting Bob Marley songs." I looked at Fisher, as if he needed the added explanation. "My brother's a whack job; his brain's fried on drugs."

"What kind?" Fisher asked.

"I don't think he discriminates. I know he does a lot of meth."

"That's hard to get up here," Fisher said, thoughtfully tapping his head with the pencil, then pointing its tip at me. "That's good info. It'll help me chase down leads, y'know?"

"And then there was the phone call," Charlie said. "Jay, tell him about the phone call."

Rita returned with a new pitcher, and we all refilled.

"While Turley was telling me they'd found Pete's body at the TC," I said, "I got a call from a guy, a boy—real soft-spoken, voice cracking— who said he'd dropped off a computer and wanted it back. Obviously, he was looking for my brother. I don't know how he got my number. He sounded desperate. He offered to pay money."

"When?"

"When, what?"

"When did you get this call?" Fisher asked.

"I already told you. When I was on my cell with Turley, yesterday. Maybe, what, Charlie? Noon? Could have been a coincidence."

"In the world of investigation," said Fisher, "there's no such thing." He jotted a note. "You received the call on your cell?"

"Yes, I was at Charlie's."

"You call the number back?"

"No. Why would I?"

Fisher exhaled. "Jesus, you guys have no idea what you're doing."

"We're not *doing* anything," I said.

"That's the problem," said Fisher. "Is the number still on your phone?"

I pulled my cell and scrolled through Saturday's calls. I recognized the police station number, so it was easy to find. Only, it was pointless.

"Restricted," I said.

"Interesting," replied Fisher. He held out his hand for my phone.

"Why do you want my phone? I told you the number was blocked."

He kept his hand out, twiddling his fingers, so I slapped the phone in his palm.

"Let a professional handle this," he said.

I don't think he noticed me rolling my eyes at Charlie. He scribbled in his notepad, before passing back my cell.

I answered some more of his questions about the bikers at the shop, my brother's recent bizarre behavior, the details of Pete's death. After another pitcher, when Fisher started slurring his words and getting snippy, I got a feeling the subject of Gina Rosinski might come up soon if I didn't bail. So I said I had to take a piss, then headed out to my truck.

Sizable drifts had started to mount in the parking lot as snow continued to fall. Letting my truck idle, I cranked the heat, even though I knew damn well it wouldn't work, then got mad when it didn't and pounded the dash.

Heading back to my place, I grew increasingly furious, livid, although at what, exactly, I couldn't be sure. Maybe for wasting the last hour and a half of my life with Fisher and Charlie, acting like a bunch of teenage Hardy Boys trying to crack the case of the missing yellow dog. I collected junk. Charlie worked for the phone company. Fisher pushed pencils and thought he was Dick Tracy. And Chris? My brother was nothing but an opportunistic scam artist who'd pissed away his life. And now he'd pissed off the wrong people and was going to have to pay the piper. There was no good end to this, and I felt guilty for admitting I'd be happier if he stayed gone. And then I knew what I was so angry about. It was a rotten thing to think about your own brother, no matter how big a fuck-up he was.

I hopped over the Turnpike, hitting the no-man's-land stretch of Orchard Drive, a long, one-lane road that ran along old apple orchards. No streetlights. No houses. Bumpy, torn-up gravel. With the storm, I couldn't see shit through the swirling gusts, my truck's rear end swinging all over the place. Drainage ditches, filled with the felled limbs of fruitless apple trees, traversed each side. The last thing you wanted out here was to blow a tire or to spin off into one of these culverts and spend the next two hours trying to wedge a jack on soft, loose soil.

I downshifted to a slog and had just lit a smoke, cleared the windshield of fog, when out of nowhere, a pair of headlights jumped in my rearview, a giant, gas-guzzling 4x4 practically crawling up my ass. I waved the driver around, but he stuck right there, glued to my bumper. I slowed down even more. Fuck it. Let the asshole ram me. I'd have an excuse to get out of my truck and beat something senseless. The guy didn't move, though, instead blasting high beams and revving the engine. Something told me this wasn't a random drunk driver. I kicked it up, my bed skidding, slipping. I put my hand up to shield the unrelenting glare from the headlights. As soon as I hit Axel Rod Road, whoever it was peeled off, headlights sweeping north.

What the hell? I might've been buzzed, but that sobered me up fast. I could feel my heart stuck in my throat.

* * *

Pulling into the filling station, trying to figure out what had just happened, I looked up and saw the lights still on in my apartment. Despite how angry I'd been at her, at that moment, I was really hoping Jenny had stuck around.

Taking two stairs at a time, I started running through all the things I wanted to say.

Then I pushed the front door open and discovered my apartment had been ransacked.

Cupboards flung open, shelves overturned, silverware strewn across the floor, chipped ceramic and shards of glass everywhere. I called for Jenny. No answer. Stepping into my bedroom, I saw my chest of drawers had all been pulled out, balls of socks and underwear spilled, flannels, jackets, my only dress shirt and suit ripped from hangers. Even my mattress had been tossed. A thorough working over. Living room, bathroom. But she wasn't here.

My first thought was trying to comprehend why anyone would want to rob me. My next immediately shot to the only person who would. Except this hadn't been my brother. Someone had been after more than spare change or trinkets to hock.

Scanning the damage in the living room, I could see my TV facedown on the carpet, books and DVDs, my entire movie collection fanned like a bad blackjack hand.

Had one of those thugs from the computer shop followed me back here? Had the guy who phoned yesterday found out where I lived? Charlie had been amped up over the hard drive. I wasn't even sure it existed. But why else would someone break in?

Then I thought about Jenny. How long had I been at the Dubliner? What if she had still been here when whoever did this showed up?

I pulled my cell to call her and saw that the porch door was open. I thought I heard stirring out there. Tucking the phone away, I crept past the closet toward the patio. I took a deep breath and jerked the handle. Something jumped at me and my hands flew up.

I looked down and saw my nameless cat rubbing against my leg, crying.

"What the hell is wrong with you?" I said. "Get in here. You're going to freeze to death."

A blur came from out of the shadows, a hard crack against the base of my skull. A searing flash of white blazed behind my eyes.

Then everything went black.

CHAPTER NINE

Deadened voices dialed in and out of reception, a radio clinging to its last taste of frequency, like that dream you have where you're drowning, clawing at the ice or trapped beneath an avalanche, muffled sound clapping in waves. A pinhole of light shone from far away, expanding into a slow ball of heat. Reaching for it, I anticipated warmth and forgiveness, some profound emotion.

Instead, I opened my eyes to Turley jabbing a penlight at my irises.

"He's all right," said Turley, with a goofy grin. He kneeled beside me, laboring with each breath the way fat men do. I sat up. My skull felt like it had been stomped by a pair of Doc Martens at a punk show.

"Whoa, big fella," Sheriff Sumner said. "Hold on. You got whacked pretty good. Wait till we can get a doctor up here to check you out." With his diminutive stature and snow-white hair, Pat Sumner reminded me of a badger from a children's book.

"I'm fine," I said.

Turley placed his hand on my chest. I shoved it away and got to my feet. I rubbed the back of my head, which lumped sticky with congealed blood.

Another uniformed cop, a young Puerto Rican kid I'd never seen before, clean-shaven with a crew cut, walked in and said something to Turley, who turned and left the apartment. The kid poked around in the kitchen, picking up and inspecting random objects, leaving me in the living room with Pat, expression awash with grandfatherly concern.

"How's your head?"

"I'm all right," I said, patting down my jeans for my cigarettes and not finding any.

The detective I'd seen at the TC stepped in from the porch, scowling as he scoured my dingy apartment and surveyed the carnage from the break-in. His face was cold and alien, void of any charm or kindness. I immediately resented him being there. It was more than the slicked hair and moisturized skin, the way he pulled off his leather gloves one finger at a time. He projected a superior disdain, like somehow just being in our hick town was beneath him.

"Can you tell me what happened?" Pat asked.

"I'd gone down to the Dubliner," I said. "When I came home, the place was torn to shit. I checked the back porch. I guess somebody was still here."

"Didn't see who?" Pat asked.

I shook my head "no."

"Have you spoken with your brother?" the big city detective asked, stepping to me without a trace of sympathy or respect for personal space.

"No," I said, pulling back, "I haven't."

He scoffed. "I find it hard to believe he wouldn't have contacted you by now."

I turned to Pat. "Who the hell is this guy?"

"Jay, this is Detective McGreevy. He's up from Concord, investigating the Pete Naginis murder."

"Yeah, well, he's in my apartment now, and I haven't seen any ID."

"Jay," Pat said with a nervous laugh, "I know you got a good bump on your head, but there's no reason to be rude."

Agitated more than offended, McGreevy whipped out his ID badge from his inner breast pocket and shoved it in my face.

Wallace D. J. McGreevy, City of Concord, Detective.

I'd heard before that you should never trust a man with two first names. Wasn't sure where conventional wisdom stood on three.

He flipped the wallet back just as fast, returning it inside his crisp overcoat. "Let's try this again. Have you spoken with your brother?"

I shook my head.

McGreevy resumed inspecting the damage, room to room, kicking aside my belongings distastefully like they were steaming turds.

"You sure you didn't get *any* look at who did this to you?" Pat asked.

"Not really. I mean, I saw an arm swing at me, but I couldn't see who it was attached to. Must've been hiding in the closet." I paused a second. "Why are you guys even here?"

"Hank heard a commotion out back," said Pat, gesturing with his thumb. "Whoever knocked you out made a helluva racket running down those old creaky steps. Hank found you passed out on the floor and called us. Turley's downstairs with him now, to see if they broke into the garage too, or if they were just targeting you."

Targeting me? I remembered the truck following me from the bar.

I lowered my voice to a whisper. "I left Jenny here when I went to the Dubliner."

Pat raised his bushy white brows.

"It's not like that," I said. "Can you check on her, though?"

"Ramon," Pat called to the Puerto Rican kid. "Have Claire call and check on Jenny Price." He turned back to me. "You sure you don't need to go to the hospital?" I shook him off. As the kid was walking out, Hank came stomping up the steps.

"Anything missing from the garage?" Pat asked him.

"Locked up tighter'n a drum," said Hank. "You okay, Jay? You know who did this?" He paused, shifting uncomfortably.

It was Pat who finally asked outright. "Think this could've been your brother?"

That caught the attention of McGreevy, who stalked out of my bedroom, waiting for my response.

I made for the kitchen, found my coat on the table, flipped it over and pulled out my Marlboro Lights.

"I don't think so," I said.

"How would you know?" asked McGreevy. "You just said you didn't see anyone."

"Because Chris wouldn't sucker punch me in the dark. He might break in and steal something, but he's not going to ambush and assault his own brother." Man, this guy was rubbing me the wrong way.

I didn't see any reason to come clean about the bikers at that computer shop or the mysterious phone call or any missing hard drive. I might've told Pat, had we been alone. But I didn't trust this McGreevy. I had no idea why a detective would be up from Concord, hanging out with our yokel police department and probing the whereabouts of a junkie, even one wanted for questioning in a murder. That's not how we did things up here. His involvement had set off my bullshit meter. Even if I couldn't figure out exactly what that meter was reading, other than he sure as hell didn't have my brother's best interest at heart. And I knew something else: this wasn't a random robbery. For as agitated as I'd been earlier, thinking Charlie was getting swept up in the drama and that Fisher's involvement was completely unnecessary, I was suddenly glad I'd made that trip to the Dubliner. I didn't have a whole lot of faith in the cops.

I went to the fridge, grabbed a beer, and pressed the cold aluminum against the back of my skull, where a sizable knot had blossomed.

Ramon returned upstairs.

"Miss Price is fine," the kid said through a heavy accent. "Left here around eleven." Anticipating the follow-up, he added, "Didn't see anything."

Pat said he'd have a prowl car patrol the neighborhood, which I told him was unnecessary, but he insisted. I soon realized that it had less to do with my safety and more to do with my brother; if he came knocking, they wanted to be nearby to pick up his ass. Even though Pat was doing most of the talking, the way McGreevy loomed over him made it clear who was running this show.

No one but me seemed convinced it hadn't been Chris who'd broken in. I'd certainly startled someone though, and there was no doubt he'd been in the middle of looking for something. It broke down to two possibilities: either it was my brother, and he'd been jonesing bad enough to coldcock me; or, that computer hard drive was real, and there was something damning enough on it that people were willing to break, enter, and assault to get it.

* * *

The telephone ringing ripped me from a deep sleep, from somewhere soundless and beyond dreaming. My head throbbed worse than any hangover I'd ever had. And I'd endured some brutal ones.

I rolled over and gripped a pillow around my ears, but whoever it was had no intention of giving up. I dragged my ass out of bed, scuffled into the kitchen, kicking aside the junkyard that was my new floor. I swiped the phone from its cradle and fell into the chair.

As soon as I put the receiver to my ear, she started in.

"You want to tell me why the police are calling my house at two a.m., asking my *boyfriend* if I arrived home safely from *your* apartment?"

Rubbing a hard hand over my face, I searched for a clock. That's another problem with the dead of winter up here, you never know what the hell time it is. The only clock in the kitchen, the one on the microwave, had stopped working when it had been jerked from the wall during the robbery. Out the window, rolling dark clouds dimmed the light. It could've been eight in the morning or nine at night. I reached out in the cold darkness for my Marlboro Lights on the table, located the pack, and clamped one with my teeth.

"What time is it?" I asked, wearily leaning over to light the cig off the stove.

"Almost noon," Jenny snapped. "What the hell have you been up to that you're still in bed at twelve o'clock in the afternoon?"

I didn't have much in this life, no fancy sound systems or nice cookware, practically every possession lifted from homes I'd cleaned for Tom, or bartered in trade at swap shops. My apartment was decorated primarily with dead people's trash, and now, spread across the tattered old carpets and stained, cracked linoleum, I saw it for what it truly was: the crap nobody else wanted.

"Are you going to answer me?" Jenny demanded. "Do you have any idea how *pissed* Brody was to be woken by the police? To learn I was over at your house at eleven o'clock at night when I should've been working? When I'd only gone there in the first place because I was so worried about—"

"I was attacked," I said, inhaling.

"What do you mean, you were 'attacked'?"

I tried to find an ashtray. The whole place was nothing but. I grabbed one of the dozen empty beer cans on the floor. "Somebody was waiting in my apartment when I got home from meeting Charlie last night. They hit me with something, knocked me out."

"Oh my God, Jay, are you all right?"

"I got a goose egg on the back of my head. But, yeah, I'm fine."

"Did you call the cops?"

"They're the ones who found me."

"Did they catch whoever it was?"

"I don't know. I mean, they hadn't when I went to bed last night."

"Who'd want to rob you?"

She didn't bring up Chris, at least not right away, even though I knew that's what she must've been thinking.

"Sorry about Brody," I said. "I told the cops to call and make sure you were all right. I didn't know if you were still here when whoever broke in. I guess I should've called myself."

"No, I'm sorry. I shouldn't have jumped down your throat like that. I'm just glad you're all right." I heard the strained exhale. "You don't think—"

"I don't think so," I said, cutting her off. "I know it sounds crazy, but I would've been able to tell if had it been my brother. For as much shit as he's pinched from me over the years, and as much grief as he's caused, clubbing me unconscious in the dark takes it to a whole new level of scumbag."

"Maybe he's getting desperate since they found his friend dead and all."

"Listen, it wasn't him. Trust me. Probably just a couple punk, high school kids. But this is only going to make the cops look harder for Chris. There's some big-shot detective up from Concord investigating." Outside, I heard an alarm that sounded like my truck. "Can you call me back in two minutes?"

"Um, sure."

I rushed to the window that overlooked the lot below, and pulled back the curtain in time to catch Hank Miller switching off an alarm to another truck in his garage. He caught a glimpse of me and sheepishly waved. I waved back.

Fuck, I was on edge.

I walked over to the TV facedown on the carpet and lifted it back on its stand, clicking the remote to see if it still worked, certain the old tubes inside had been shattered. Surprisingly, Channel 3's *News at Noon* switched on. Another report about the ski industry up here, footage of folks hitting the slopes, some perky blonde reporter in a neon-pink parka, flashing a blinding megawatt smile. Skiing was a lucrative business in New Hampshire, attracting the vacationing jet set across New England. Though the nearest resort was an hour away, Ashton was in the heart of the mountains, and you'd see packed minivans with glistening racks on the highway and Turnpike all season long. Must be nice. You bust your ass to stay up on child support payments, scraping by to keep food on your plate and a goddamn roof over your head, and you don't have much time leftover for playing in the snow. The perky blonde cut to a clip featuring Ashton's favorite son, Adam Lombardi, in a hard hat. I went to turn up the sound when the phone rang.

"Everything okay?" Jenny asked.

"It's nice that you're so worried about me."

On the TV, they were back on the slopes, where an all-American family in coordinated outfits was being interviewed. I switched it off. No wonder I rarely watched the goddamn thing. If it wasn't sports or a movie, television only made me mad.

"Of course, I worry," Jenny said. "I told you that last night."

"When you were at my apartment. At almost midnight." I laughed. "Brody must've loved that."

"You have *no* idea," she said, laughing back.

"I think I do. If you were my girl over some other guy's house—"

"That's the thing, Jay. You're not just 'some other guy.' You know how hard that is for Brody?"

I wanted to say, "You know how little I give a fuck?" But I didn't. "How's our son?"

"He's with my mom. She's taking him to her sewing group."

"Poor guy."

"You kidding me? All those old ladies pinching his cheeks and giving him treats? I know you don't like her much, but I'm glad he has at least one grandparent in his life. I don't know what I'd do without her."

"I like your mom just fine," I said. "She doesn't like me. Listen, I'm not working right now. I mean, I still have a job, but Tom is laying low for a while. I can help out watching Aiden more during the day, if you need me to."

"He's your son. You can see him anytime you'd like. But my mom has the time and, frankly, I'm not sure I'd feel good with Aiden over at your place with what's been going on. After what you just told me, I don't feel too good with *you* being at your place."

"Don't worry about me," I said. "I'm a big boy. I'm sorry for any headache with Brody last night. Blame it all on me if you need to."

Jenny giggled. "What do you think I did?"

CHAPTER TEN

I called Charlie to see if he had time for lunch at the Olympic Diner. As luck would have it, he said, he was wrapping up a service call down the road and would meet me there.

The Olympic was on the south end of the Desmond Turnpike, which connected bigger counties like Colebrook and Pittsfield, so it attracted more foot traffic than the rest of town. We'd practically lived at the twenty-four-hour diner in high school, every party eventually finding its way there come dawn.

Sitting in the parking lot, I drank the coffee I'd picked up across the street at the Shell station, smoking from a fresh pack of cigarettes, waiting for Charlie. The streets were paved, but you couldn't scrape up all the snow and ice, each passing storm only adding a layer to the asphalt permafrost.

A slick sheen glistened off everything, long icicles dripping from electrical lines, Ashton consumed by deep, dark gray. Tall weeds and bramble reeds poked through the hard snow, creeping and cracking around streetlamps, bumpers and barriers, like crippled beanstalks.

This section of the Turnpike seemed more respectable, with businesses and restaurants like Best Buy, Jiffy Lube, Friendly's—there was even a duckpin bowling alley where I attended birthday parties as a kid—but in between all the department outlets and national chains were still the places no one really wanted to be: cheap motels, dollar stores, military surplus shacks, knickknack and consignment shops, The Salvation Army, fast food drive-throughs, all-night gas stations.

I watched the stragglers. Not bums, exactly. That wouldn't be fair to say. But hardly upstanding citizens. It was pushing one o'clock on a weekday afternoon, and the boulevard bustled with activity. Didn't anybody work? Almost always in pairs, they seemed to wander without direction. They were vagrants, welfare recipients who lived in one of the countless dumpy hotels that populated this stretch, waiting for their next public handout to get high and fuck away the pain, the lost kids, the alcoholic men and broken-down women, the easily forgotten and the quickly replaced.

I remembered buying pot years ago off a guy who lived in one of these motels. He couldn't have been much older than I am now, but he seemed incomprehensibly old at the time. I could still picture the inside of that hellhole as he weighed the bud on an old-fashioned, balance-beam scale—warbling game show on a tiny black and white TV with rabbit ears; the near-naked, emaciated woman laying on the unmade bed; the ribbons of blue smoke that floated like cirrus clouds in a lazy summer sky—thinking I couldn't get out of there fast enough.

For as much time as I'd spent on the Turnpike and in the diner when I was younger, these sights and sounds never before completely registered. I didn't understand how someone could tolerate a single day of it, let alone years. And that's how my brother had lived most of his life.

A knock on my passenger-side window startled me, and I looked up to see Charlie mugging against the glass.

* * *

"You were kind of a dick last night," Charlie said inside the diner. We sat in a booth against the long pane window, overlooking the Turnpike. Each booth came with its own miniature jukebox. We were about the only ones in there, having missed the lunch crowd.

"Fisher hates my guts." I flipped through the selections on the jukebox, nothing more recent than the 1980s, and not the good shit, either. The best you could hope for was maybe Hall & Oates, a "Little Red Corvette," a Michael Jackson song before his face turned entirely plastic. The diner did its best to maintain the illusion of nostalgia, which was its primary appeal. That and the waitresses. Certainly wasn't the food.

"You shouldn't have felt up his girlfriend," said Charlie.

"*A,* she wasn't his girlfriend, and *B,* that was fifteen years ago. How long does someone hold onto a grudge?"

"You tell me. Guy's trying to do you a favor. You might be a little more appreciative."

"Someone broke into my place last night."

The waitress, a beautiful, young Greek girl with long, straight black hair and the type of face they write poetry about, came to take our order. Her family had owned the restaurant since I was a kid, and it seemed they never ran out of beautiful, young waitresses. An endless parade. Every time you stepped into the Olympic, there was another gorgeous Greek girl in a tight blue skirt, ready to offer service with a smile.

"Who?" Charlie asked, after he'd ordered a burger with the works and she'd strutted away.

"Huh?"

"Stop ogling the help. Who broke into your apartment?"

I hadn't ordered anything, just coffee, my gut acting up, which didn't make coffee the smartest bet, I knew, but I was dragging ass and needed to get it in gear.

"Beats me," I said, grabbing a fistful of sugar packets and emptying them in the faded brown mug. "I walked in on them. Cracked me good on the back of the head. Cops found me out cold. And don't ask if it was my brother. I'm sick of the question. Chris couldn't drop me with a hockey stick and a running start."

"Actually, I was thinking it was those guys from the computer shop."

"Possible," I said. "Didn't take anything, whoever it was. Tore the place to hell looking for something, though."

The waitress returned with the pot and filled me up, smiling awkwardly when our conversation halted as soon as she came near.

"That hard drive," whispered Charlie after she'd left. "I told you." He stabbed his finger at me. "That's the key to this whole thing."

"I'm not ready to go all in on that yet. We're basing everything we know on the ramblings of a drug addict—a drug addict who believes, among other things, that our country was founded by aliens and that the government poisons our drinking water. My brother is a lunatic. And a liar. When Chris speaks, you have to divide by four."

"Pete Naginis is dead. Murdered. Or have you forgotten that?"

"They live a rough life, stealing, shooting drugs, getting in debt to the wrong people."

Charlie held up a hand and started ticking off items, using each finger to illustrate his point. "Your brother's missing. That detective's up from Concord. The phone call? Those gangbangers at the shop? And now somebody breaks into your apartment? That's gotta add up to something, don't you think?"

"I don't know what to think, Charlie." I peered out through the cold glass, at the cars and trucks zooming along the wet road. "That detective's name's McGreevy. He was at my place with Turley and Pat last night. Tell you one thing. I don't like the guy. He's playing some angle."

"You want to crash at my place for a few? Maybe whoever it was will come back. I wouldn't want those biker methheads catching *me* at home alone." I could see by the sudden change in expression that he'd just made the connection. "Shit, I was with you."

"I wouldn't worry about it. If someone is looking for that hard drive, my apartment makes sense, yours doesn't. Plus, I'm not totally convinced it was those guys from the shop."

"Who, then?"

"I don't know," I said. "But if my brother wasn't blowing smoke and this isn't all a bizarre coincidence, there has to be something pretty damning in those files."

"Did he have the hard drive with him at your place?"

"Not unless it fit inside his filthy brown backpack."

"So, Pete had it?"

"My guess."

"And now Pete's dead."

The pretty Greek waitress brought Charlie's burger, which he immediately began doctoring—salting, peppering, slathering in sauce.

I watched the waitress wriggle away in her tight blue skirt. Nineteen, twenty. Man, I was only ten years removed from that age and I might as well have been a hundred years old.

"Maybe Fisher will turn up something," Charlie said, chomping down on his burger, gobs of mustard, mayo, and ketchup squirting out the sides and dribbling over his fingers.

"If you talk to him, tell him sorry. I was a little high-strung last night."

"No worries," said Charlie, through the wad of masticated hamburger mash. "So, what's the plan now? Head back to that computer shop?" He snorted at his own joke.

"Maybe later." I gazed at the roaming nomads schlepping through the roadside slush. "My brother has to be around here somewhere."

Charlie sucked the meat juices off his thumb.

"We don't have any soup kitchens or shelters in town," I said. "Maybe he's over in Pittsfield. But that's a long haul just for a place to sleep. I know he crashes at some of these motels on the Turnpike when he gets enough money." I gestured out the window. "There is this one girl he used to hang around with, Kitty something."

"Kitty?"

"That's how he introduced her to me. Kitty. Used to bring her around a lot. Shit, this was, like, a couple years ago. I normally don't pay attention to any of his friends, they come and go so fast, but she seemed to mean more to him than most of the ones he runs around with."

"Girlfriend?"

"I'm not sure guys like my brother have girlfriends. Anyway, she stopped coming by. Hardly a prize, as strung-out as him. She had a room in a boarding house over in Middlebury. Middle of fucksake nowhere. Had me drop her off there once."

"Who lives in a boarding house? What is this? The 1940s?"

I shrugged.

"Why haven't you checked there before now?"

"Because it was three fucking years ago," I said. "I doubt she even still lives there."

"I thought you said it was two years."

"I don't know, Charlie. Maybe it was two. Maybe it was a year. It's been a while, though. I haven't given it much thought until now. Why would I? I have my own fucking life, y'know?" Out the window, a bum struggled to keep from slipping as he pushed a shopping cart across the icy parking lot. "You don't understand what's it's been like dealing with my brother."

"I think I have a good idea."

"He's like a child. You can't take his plans or his friends seriously. Everyone he hangs around with is like that. They all live in a fantasy world, as whacked out as he is."

Charlie's phone on the table started to vibrate. He checked it, glumly muttering, then hopped up and extracted a wad of bills from his hip pocket. "Gotta run. Call me this afternoon. Let me know what you find." He left a ten-spot, slipped on his work coat, then shoved the last bite of bacon and burger down his gullet. "And I mean it, if you want to crash at my place, got an extra bed and everything."

I nodded my appreciation. He double knocked on the table and hurried out the door.

* * *

Buried deep in the valley cuts, Middlebury oozed so much backwoods' backwater it made Ashton seem like a bustling metropolis. Small, spread-out dairy farms and gummed-up slaughterhouses, broken-down harvesters rusting in untended fields, distant houses where the top floor lights never went out. Murders of big black crows perched high in treetops, suspiciously eyeing strangers. They'd wait for the shotgun blasts to echo in the distance, before scattering in fifteen different directions.

At the end of a tortuously long, one-lane road that carved through granite gullies and dense thicket in the rugged northern outback, Middlebury's town center comprised a tiny grocery market, a gas station with one pump, and a restaurant that closed at two in the afternoon. That was it. Even by rural standards, Middlebury was Hicksville.

The people who lived in Middlebury fell into one of two camps: radical militia types who didn't like the government telling them what to do, so they stockpiled firearms and refurbished land mines, collected canned goods by the crate-load, burrowing deep underground, prepping for doomsday. You'd spot them on patrol, making rounds, trolling compound perimeters in camouflage fatigues, sporting subterranean tans like extras from *The Hills Have Eyes*, hoping for some poor bastard to mistakenly wander onto their property.

Then there were the rehabilitated.

I knew of at least two halfway houses and one transitional living facility. I guess they thought by sticking addicts in the middle of nowhere it would be harder for them to score dope or get drunk. But if my brother had taught me one thing about addiction, it was that when an addict wants to get high, ain't hell or high water going to stop him.

Back when I'd try to fix my brother, a doctor mentioned these homes as possible landing points, should Chris manage to stay sober long enough to warrant transitional housing. He never made it past twenty-seven days.

I wouldn't have known the boarding house existed at all, had my brother not roped me into dropping off his girlfriend late one night. Took forever. The farther the road stretched, the longer I knew it would take to get back, and the more enraged I'd become. The girl, Kitty, tried being friendly, attempting to strike up a conversation, undeterred by my lack of response. Which only made me seethe more. What could she and I possibly have to talk about?

Who'd choose to live in a boarding house anyway, especially one so far off the beaten path? Public transportation didn't run in these parts. These people never had their own car. It was like self-imposed exile. Hell, even the *idea* of a boarding house struck me as odd, like a leftover relic from a World War II love story, a sailor down on his luck in an old film noir. Who couldn't get their shit together enough to at least rent a goddamn motel room on the Turnpike?

* * *

I steered down the wooded drive, and the boarding house, a once-grand, two-story American Colonial, rose into view. I'd dropped Kitty off in the middle of the night that first time, and I hadn't gotten much of a look. With its sprawling acreage and tree-lined entrance, the home might've passed for a plantation in the 1700s, if shutters weren't dangling by their hinges, and weeds and vines hadn't choked everything. Tall, white columns framed a long rocking porch, where, despite late-afternoon, frigid winds, five old ladies sat shawled in rocking chairs. Wrapped in cheap-looking coats, hidden beneath Goodwill hats, each smoked a cigarette with frail, palsied hands.

When I exited my truck and slammed shut the door, the women collectively jumped, before clustering together and staring, wide-eyed.

As I drew closer, I realized I'd been mistaken. These weren't old women—they were girls, barely out of their teens.

The porch door flung open, and a big-boned, sturdy, middle-aged woman bundled in flannel and dungarees, bulled down the unpainted steps. "You can't be here!" she barked, marching toward me, meaty paws rolling over a dishtowel.

"I'm looking for someone," I said.

"Well, this ain't the place to be looking!" She grabbed my elbow and began dragging me off the grounds.

"Hey!" I said, trying to shake free. "What are you doing?"

She didn't answer, didn't stop, just plowed ahead like a determined, gruff tugboat. When I planted my boots and refused to take another step, she clamped onto my forearms and drove her shoulder into my flank, like she planned to check me into the boards. I'd had enough.

I shoved her away. "Get your fucking hands off me!"

The girls on the porch gasped, trembling like Amish virgins who'd never seen a man before.

"Go inside, girls," the woman said, calmly but firmly, as though practicing a rehearsed fire drill.

The girls remained frozen, gawking with spooked eyes, skittish as underfed alley cats. I wondered if this was a home for mentally handicapped people or something.

"Go inside," the woman repeated, only this time more firmly, and, one by one, the timid things shuffled through the door like pious church mice.

I felt bad, although I didn't know why. I hadn't done anything wrong. This woman had practically assaulted me. Still, I felt the need to explain myself.

"I'm looking for a friend of mine," I said. "If you could tell me—"

"You made a big mistake coming here. You have ten seconds to get in your truck and drive off before I call the cops!"

"Call the cops? For what? Asking if somebody is home? What the hell is your problem, lady? I'm just trying to find my brother's ex-girlfriend. He's missing. I thought he might be staying at the boarding house with her. Or that she might've at least seen him."

Lips pursed, hands at the ready like she was prepared to take a swing at me, the woman cocked her head, curiously. The anger slowly drained from her red, pudgy face. "Boarding house?" she said, dropping her shoulders. "What do you think this is, 1940? This is a battered women's shelter."

"Oh, shit." Showing up in a giant, rumbling truck, storming up the walkway, barking that I wasn't leaving. The exact scene these women needed sheltering from. "I'm sorry. I didn't know."

"Now you do. So, please, leave."

I showed my hands. "Listen, my brother really is missing."

"I'm sorry to hear that," she said, "but you still need to leave."

"He has a drug problem."

"That's terrible. A lot of these girls are fleeing that world. But I need you to leave, now."

"They just found a friend of his dead at the TC truck stop. He'd been murdered. I don't know where else to look. Please. Help me."

The wind whipped around us as the last glimmer of light disappeared behind the tall trees.

"Can we sit in my truck for a few seconds and talk?" I immediately backtracked. "I'm really not looking to cause any problems. I'm a nice guy, I swear. Maybe you know my brother? Chris Porter? I dropped off his girlfriend here once. A long time ago. Like, maybe two years. It's why I thought this was a boarding house. That's what they told me. And I believed them."

"Son, I'm sure you're a nice guy. It was a misunderstanding, okay? No hard feelings. But you have to leave. I can't tell you who's here. Don't you know that's the whole point of a house like this? Nobody should know it exists. Why else would we be in the middle of nowhere? I don't know who would've asked you to bring them here, since that girl should've known that."

"Her name was Kitty."

The name must've registered, because her expression instantly changed, though for better or worse, I couldn't say.

I pulled out my wallet. I carried business cards for hauling that Tom had had printed. They showed a cartoon man in a hard hat, standing beside a dump truck, giving an enthusiastic thumbs up. I hated the damn things, but passed one along anyway. She reluctantly plucked it from my fingers, squinting down at the goofy logo.

"I know you can't tell me if she's here." I started backing up to my truck. "But maybe you can have her call me? I swear, I'm telling the truth. I'm not some domestic-abusing jerk or anything like that. I'm just a guy looking for his brother. I'm worried about him. If you see Kitty, give her my card, okay? Use it to check out who I am first. Call the Ashton PD. They'll verify everything I've told you."

As I threw my truck in reverse, I saw her tuck away the card and stalk back into the house. She didn't wave goodbye.

* * *

Driving back, darkness strangling the countryside, no moon, not a single star in the winter sky to guide my way home, I lit a cigarette and watched my breath cloud in the glowing dashboard lights.

I felt terrible for how I'd acted at the women's shelter, like some knuckle-dragging troglodyte. I started rehashing all my other stupid missteps and cringe-worthy lapses in my life, which is how things happened: one mistake begetting another, building a lifetime's worth of regret—a snowball effect.

I realized now why I'd snapped at Charlie over lunch. He was right. I hadn't been doing my best to find Chris. I knew I resented my brother, but I didn't appreciate just how much I'd grown to hate him. I hadn't bothered trying to track down Kitty or any of his other friends because a part of me wanted him to stay gone.

When I got back into town, without really thinking about it, I headed for Lamentation Bridge. I stood in front of my truck.

Engine rumbling, high beams backlighting me, midnight winds howling. I skimmed rocks off the ice and felt the big clock winding down.

* * *

By the time I pulled into Hank Miller's lot, I'd smoked half a pack of cigarettes and pinched a nerve in my neck throwing too many stones. Too scatterbrained to see the police cruiser waiting for me until I was practically on top of it, I had to hammer on the brakes to keep from rear-ending Turley.

As soon he stepped out and I saw his face, I knew it was about Chris.

CHAPTER ELEVEN

"Tried calling you," said Turley, tugging on the furred earflaps of his brown police hat. "Someone spotted your brother." He jammed his hands into his coat pockets.

"He's okay?" I asked, although it was less a question for Turley, and more for my own ears to hear. "Where is he?"

"On the run," said Turley. "Got caught breaking into Gerry Lombardi's house."

"Gerry Lombardi?" Why the hell would he break into his old wrestling coach's house?

"Lombardi's wife, Camille, called it in. Gerry's with the team down in Manchester for the tournament. Regionals."

Of all the houses to break into. "She's sure it was Chris?"

"Yup. Startled the hell out of her too. Knows your brother well from his days wrestling with Adam. She'd been having dinner with a friend in town, came home, saw the light on in Gerry's office, walked in and caught your brother, red-handed, rifling through Gerry's desk. She said he looked like a wild animal. Filthy, smelled bad, like he'd been sleeping in the woods."

As if anybody could last a night in this cold. "Why would Chris be rummaging through Mr. Lombardi's desk?"

"Gerry's pretty old," said Turley. "Got that bad back. Chris must've thought he had some painkillers lying around." Turley pointed into the night. "Got a car prowling Elton Drive and Axel Rod Road right now. Can't imagine he'd get far. I've been camped by your door in case he showed up."

"He's not coming here with you guys looking for him."

"Probably not," said Turley. "But I figured I could at least let you know he's alive. Thought you'd like to hear that."

I was surprised at how much I actually did.

Turley zipped his padded coat to the neck and gave another quick shiver. He glanced up at the overcast sky. "Supposed to get another foot tonight."

"I heard. Thanks. I mean, for letting me know."

Turley touched the brim of his furred cap, then retreated inside his car. He unrolled the window. "Don't worry," he said, "we'll find your brother. And we'll bring him in safe." Turley hit the lights, which had to be for my benefit since there was no one else around.

Reds and blues swirling, he spun his tires, spitting up gravel, taillights receding into the distance.

* * *

I called Charlie as soon as I got upstairs, but his cell went straight to voice mail. I began to leave a message, then stopped. Fuck it, I'll head down to the Dubliner. You could find the guy at the bar practically every night.

I put out some food for my fat, nameless cat, plucked a T-shirt that didn't smell too bad off the floor, and was about to walk out the door when Charlie called back.

"Hey, Charlie," I said, slipping on my coat. "You'll never believe this. Mrs. Lombardi saw him."

"Jay?" a voice responded. Only it wasn't Charlie. It was a woman.

"Who is this?"

"Katherine," the woman said. "Friends used to call me 'Kitty.'"

I patted down my pockets for my cigarettes, fumbling to pull one out and get it lighted. I didn't know why the call was making me so nervous.

"Jolene said you stopped by this afternoon?"

"Jolene?" I waved out the match head. "Oh, the woman from the shelter, right?" My cat rubbed its fat, furry belly against my pant leg.

"You told her your brother was missing? Is that who they saw?"

"When?"

"Just now. You said, 'Charlie, someone saw him.' Did you mean Chris?"

"Sorry. Yes. I did." She was speaking to me like we were familiar, friends even; that's what was throwing me off. "You remember me?" I asked. Aside from that one night giving Kitty a ride to the shelter, I hadn't spent a lot of time in her company, and probably hadn't uttered six words to her, total. Even on that drive, I didn't recall having been particularly nice.

Kitty laughed uneasily. "I knew more *of* you. Chris talked about you. A lot."

"He did? What did he say?" I figured if Chris had been saying anything about me, he'd be talking shit. By the time he was hanging out with Kitty, I'd stopped giving him cash, and we fought most the time. I knew I wasn't high on his favorite people's list.

"He thought of you more as a son than he did a little brother, let's put it that way. Very protective. Chris saw it as his job to take care of you."

Only in my brother's topsy-turvy world could he see himself as my caretaker.

I heard rustling on the other line and a hand cupping the receiver, whispers to wait a minute.

"I don't mean to be rude," Kitty said, "but my shift is starting." Then, as if I'd automatically assume that meant taking the stage at a strip club somewhere—which I had—she threw in, "I'm a hostess. At a restaurant. In California. I don't live at the shelter anymore. I'm clean now. Thirty-nine months. I live with my sister."

"That's good," I said.

"Thanks to your brother. He's the one who put me on the bus."

"My brother?" Chris hadn't kept a checking account in fifteen years. How the hell was he helping anyone else?

"He's got a big heart, your brother. I was in a bad situation when I met him. This guy . . ." I could tell she was searching for the right words, like she wanted to share more, but all she said was, "Well, I'm glad you found him."

"Actually, we didn't find him. Chris is in trouble. The cops are looking for him."

"Oh. I'm sorry to hear that."

"It's a big misunderstanding. But, it's better if I find him first. I know it's been a while."

"Almost four years."

"No, really? That long?"

"I know my clean date. It's kind of a big deal. Plus, it's my daughter's birthday." More rustling. The clatter of stacked dishes, orders barked. "I really do have to run. You have my number. Call me tomorrow. We can talk some more."

"I need to find him now, Kitty. Katherine. He's got to be sleeping somewhere. He'd freeze to death up here. Any idea where he could be crashing? Anyone who might be taking him in? Whatever you can tell me would be helpful. I'm flying blind."

She paused. "Maybe one of his johns?"

"Johns?"

"Y'know, the guys he goes with?"

"My brother's gay?"

"I don't think so." She laughed uneasily. "But when you live that way, you do what you got to do to survive, y'know? When I knew him, there were a number of men who would, um, pay for his services, and in exchange they'd feed him, give him a bed to sleep in, a place to shower."

"Did he have regulars? Do you know any of their names?"

"Sorry. Listen, this is my cell. If you want to talk some more, call me tomorrow. I'll try to think of anything else. Chris helped me out of a bad situation; I'd like to repay the favor. But, honestly, I don't know much more than that. I haven't spoken with him in a long, long time." She sighed. "Good luck. I hope you find him."

"Hold on. Wait. Do you know where he'd meet these guys?"

"The truck stop."

The line went dead.

* * *

As soon as I set the phone down, it rang right back. Jenny. Calling to see how I was holding up. I said more than I should have, and felt bad about unloading on her afterwards. She asked if there was anything she could do. I told her I didn't want to get her in any more trouble with Brody. Besides, what could she really do?

I found Charlie drinking at the Dubliner. Half a fist submerged in a bowl of nuts, the other one wrapped around a nearly empty pint, eyes glued on the final moments of the Bruins game. He was the only one sitting at the bar. No surprise, with another monster snowstorm already unleashing its fury. A good couple inches had fallen just since I left my apartment. And it was only going to get worse.

I shook off the barmaid, Rita, when she started to head in my direction. Charlie turned, saw me, then motioned to her with two fingers anyway.

I tried to say "never mind," but he frantically waved his hand until the final seconds ticked off and the horn blew.

"Fuck," he muttered.

The Bruins had lost another one.

He quickly got over it. "What's up?"

"Someone saw Chris."

"No shit? Who?"

"Camille Lombardi. At her house."

"Mrs. Lombardi?" Charlie's face screwed up. "What the hell's he doing at his old wrestling coach's house?"

"Broke into Gerry's office. Camille walked in on Chris rifling through desk drawers. Turley thinks he was looking for prescription pills."

"Hmm," said Charlie. I couldn't tell if that meant he was buying the explanation or what. "That's good, right? I mean, at least he's alive and in town."

I gazed around the abandoned bar as Rita wordlessly set two pints before us.

"You want to take a ride with me?" I asked.

"Where to?"

"I'll fill you in on the way."

"What about our beers?"

"You might as well get going, Charlie," Rita chimed in. "I'm about to lock up this place. They'll be grounding the plows soon."

"You could've told me that before you let me buy the beers," Charlie said.

"Don't worry," Rita said. "It's on the house."

She went to snatch back the beers, but Charlie playfully slapped her wrist. He shot me his cat-with-a-canary grin, and downed most of his pint in one long gulp. "Let's go," he said, suds slipping down his chin.

* * *

"You're brother's a fag?" Charlie asked.

I turned the truck north onto the Turnpike, past Duncan Pond, which was famous up here for having a crane sticking out of the water. Been there since forever. This time of year, the pond was a slab of ice, but you could still see the tip of the boom and its sheave, hoist line dangling, parts rusted, thrusting out of the water like a redneck Excalibur. Nobody knew how that crane had come to rest in the middle of Duncan Pond. Rumor was, back in the early days of Lombardi Construction, a worker had gotten pissed off and sank the machine in protest. Whether that was true or just small town legend, who knew, but it was nice to chalk one up for the little guy.

"Jay?"

"Beats me, Charlie," I said, punching the lighter on the dash. "Who cares if he is?"

"I don't *care*. Just weird, is all. Your brother had so many girls back in the day."

"Kitty, Katherine, said he'd meet guys at the truck stop and they'd help him out. So that's where we're going to look." As uncomfortable as it made me to think of my brother that way, it also made sense. Someone had to be putting Chris up all these years, especially in the coldest months. Being homeless in northern New Hampshire wasn't the same as going alfresco in Arizona or Florida. What else did Chris have to offer in exchange? Nothing in this life comes free.

"Who's he go with?" Charlie asked. "Like, what, queer truckers?"

"Gay truckers. Gay lawyers. Gay whoever." I stabbed the hot, cherry end of the dashboard lighter to my cigarette and sucked in the sizzle. "How am I supposed to know how this shit works?"

"Sorry, man," said Charlie. "I know this must suck, hearing this shit about your own brother."

I flipped the wipers on high as snow and ice pelted the windshield like spitballs from a juvenile god. When Nor'easters hit, everything could grind to a halt. Once it got bad enough, the town would stop sending the plows. Then you weren't going anywhere. Forecast didn't have it letting up till morning. Which made it a lousy time to be prowling the TC in search of clues, but I didn't see how holing up in my apartment and waiting for the skies to clear was going to help the situation.

A giant, orange plow thundered past, going in the other direction. We still had a couple hours. I hoped.

As we climbed the last hill before the TC, Charlie peered over. "What's the plan, Hoss? We knock on every window? See who's feeling lonely?"

"You check out the Maple. I'll poke around the semis. If we see anyone who looks like they'd associate with my brother, we ask questions." Charlie looked like he wanted to laugh. I threw up my hands. "I don't know, man. I'm new at this investigating stuff."

"I'm busting your balls." Charlie hugged himself. "When are you going to get the fucking heater fixed in this thing? You live above a service station, for Christ's sake."

"Don't remind me."

The Travel Center was its own little town, rising like Reno from the barren tundra. Even at this hour, the place was frenzied with truck drivers pulling in and out, grizzled, road-weary warriors disembarking their big rigs to fill up on diesel at the gas station, fuel up on deep-fried at the restaurant. These were all gruff-looking men's men, with hewn, rough features, leathered lines, and unkempt facial hair. It was hard to pick out who might swing for the other team. Honestly, none of them looked much in the mood for any kind of company.

Because of the storm, they'd sectioned off most of the parking lot to keep clear for plowing, all cars corralled in a tiny square outside the restaurant. The truckers were still granted the eastern retaining wall, where dozens of semis currently were lined up, butted against the main building and extending farther than the eye could see. We parked outside the Peachtree with the rest of the tourists, which were understandably fewer given the conditions, as booming engines roared past. Whether idling or powering down, the rigs still rumbled the ground beneath your feet hundreds of yards away.

I watched as heavily flannelled men stalked into the laundry or showering facilities, or stocked up inside the convenience store, skulking back out with chubby paper sacks stuffed with Red Bulls or MiniThins, or whatever other stimulant they'd scored. I didn't see much haggling for companionship going on. Not sure where that stuff went down, exactly. I imagined they had to be discreet about it. I didn't see how that was even possible. First off, you had all the employees who worked there, maintenance and grounds personnel, waitresses and busboys, night clerks, cashiers, security guards. Plus all the travelers coming from or heading to Canada, stopping for gas and bathroom breaks, a midnight snack, screaming kids in tow. The place was crawling with people, even on a night like this, infested with all kinds, everyone scurrying to get back behind the wheel before the roads were shut down. I scanned for my brother, or, more accurately, anyone who looked the part. From inside my truck cab, I didn't see anyone who fit the bill.

I opened my wallet and pulled out an old picture of Chris and me, taken not long after our folks had died. In it, Chris was about forty pounds heavier, still had his teeth, and didn't look like he'd just stuck his head in a lawn mower. I gave it to Charlie. It was all I had.

"What do you want me to do with this?" he asked, taking the photo from me and staring at it. "Jesus, you look like a baby."

"Show it to people. Ask if anyone's seen him. Try the motor lodge next door first, ask the desk clerk, any riffraff you see slinking in the shadows. I'll try the store, then go down that row of trucks."

"Your brother don't look anything like this anymore, y'know." Charlie stared at the picture. "Hell, he looks like . . . a normal person."

"Best I can do, man. Just say you're looking for a friend who's missing. I'll meet you at the Peachtree in half an hour."

Despite the storm and the late hour, the TC still bustled, the snow really coming down now, visibility only a few feet. I wrapped my wool coat tighter around me as I made my way past the restaurant windows. Helmet-haired waitresses, all looking like variations of Flo from the old *Alice* TV show, poured coffee and slung hash, ringing up tabs with fried-hair sass. A family, taking a break from the road, shoveled in food. Mom, dad, two little boys. All wore matching white sweatshirts with giant red maple leafs. They looked so happy to be together, warm and indoors.

The Peachtree led into the Travel Center lobby, exiting by a row of arcade games and bank of pay phones, clearly leftover from a time when people actually used pay phones. Restrooms and showers splintered down the hall, running past vending, soda, and ATM machines. Another set of doors led from the lobby into the convenience store, which was more like a Walmart, so much stuff in there.

Place was huge, offering everything from groceries, to a well-stocked automotive section, and, of course, skiing accessories. Skiing and snowboarding were a big deal up here, with the Black Mountain Resort only sixty minutes away.

The lights from the gas station island burned like a thousand stars, blinding through the windows and illumining the aisles, which I prowled, keeping an eye peeled for truckers and other customers and—I wasn't entirely sure what I was looking for, but, like art or irony, I figured I'd know it when I saw it.

Shoppers were growing scarce. A few employees stocked shelves with the cheery disposition of anyone stuck working the night shift in the middle of a snowstorm, on their knees or perched on ladders, barely acknowledging my presence, except to scowl uninvitingly and make it clear not to ask any questions.

I filled a coffee and bought a pack of Marlboros, then headed south into the swirling gusts and snowfall.

The south exit opened up to the far back edge of the complex, which is where they'd found Pete Naginis' body floating face-down in the runoff. I walked to the edge of the embankment, and peered down the culvert into the rippling black water cutting through ice crusts.

The violence of Pete's death finally hit me. Until then, his murder had been a minor plot detail in someone else's story. Standing there, so close to where they'd found him, I could only imagine what those final moments must've been like for him, having someone beat you so savagely that you can't defend yourself, the helplessness, the hopelessness of knowing that no one's coming to save you. What it must truly feel like to be alone.

I lit a cigarette, thinking of the ghosts I was running from, and made for the long row of tractor-trailers along the retaining wall. Truckers passed by, ball caps pulled low, shielding their eyes, rubbing the five-day scruff, scrubbing away life on the road. Didn't even peek my way.

It would help if I knew what I was trying to find. Through the mounting snow, I didn't see any junkies or truckers exchanging money for drugs, or blowing one another in the shadows. I found no one sneaking into the backs of rigs, and I guessed, when I really thought about it, I hadn't much expected to. Prostitutes aren't trolling parking lots in the middle of a goddamn Nor'easter.

I walked the entire length of those slumbering semis, which easily ran the length of a couple football fields, pushing so far south that by the time I'd reached the end, most of the blazing light behind me had faded from view, the complex all but a soft, haloed ring, a distant moon. I was just turning around to go meet Charlie, hoping maybe he'd had better luck, when he called on my cell.

"What's up?" I asked. "I'm headed back to the Peachtree to meet you."

"Don't," he said. "Come to the Maple Motor Inn next door. Room 14. Hurry."

"Why? What'd you find?"

"Hurry," he said, dropping his voice to a whisper. "You've got to see this."

"Well, give me a minute. I'm way at the other end, past the trucks." I began hoofing it, winds assaulting, making it difficult to move or breathe. My eyes teared up, nearly stopping me in my tracks. "I'm glad you found something, because . . . Charlie?"

I checked my cell. The call had dropped.

I did my best to cover ground. Getting back to the main building took forever. I retraced my footsteps through the store and lobby, emerging in front of the Peachtree. The restaurant jutted out, concealing the motor lodge, which was still a short trek up the hill and access road.

I'd just started across the parking lot when a pair of huge snow plows arrived, dropping their straight-blade loaders to the pavement and scraping the tarmac, cutting me off, blasting my eardrums, and blocking my view as they circled around me a few times.

What had Charlie found? I stumbled across the courtyard, clomping snowy boots, past the darkened check-in office and the first thirteen rooms, all the way to number 14, which curled around the corner into the woods, where a railroad tie fence was missing half its ties.

I knocked. No one answered. I knocked harder. Nothing.

The curtains were open. I cupped my hands and peered through the glass, squinting into darkness.

There was no one there.

CHAPTER TWELVE

It hadn't taken me more than seven, ten minutes to get to the Maple Motor Inn. Maybe twelve, tops. Certainly not long enough that Charlie would've grown tired of waiting and up and split. But he wasn't there. I called his name, knocked louder, which was pointless since I could see inside. Entire room was the size of my kitchen. There'd be nowhere to hide except under the bed. Maybe I'd misheard him or gotten the room number wrong. I scanned the courtyard and the rest of the units, all dark, and then out into the snow, the wild blustery gale yielding little. No lights on in the yard, no lights on in any rooms. He'd definitely said "Room 14." Where the hell could he be? I pulled my cell and tried him again. Straight to voice mail.

The Maple Motor Inn was its own separate business and technically not part of the TC, even though traffic clearly spilled over from one to the other. Because of the snow and its location, the motor lodge, which was arranged in the classic U-shaped, auto-court style from the 1950s, hadn't provided the best view as I walked up, and I'd been unable to see the far side of the building where the soda and ice machines and actual rooms were. But Charlie couldn't have waltzed past me, which meant he'd have to have left via car, and not from the main lot, either. The entire way back, I'd seen just one set of headlights pulling in for gas.

There was another, smaller parking area obscured by the lodge that was specifically for the Maple, up an embankment and big enough only for a few cars.

I trekked up the little hill. There were several footprints, shapeless from slippage on the incline, and therefore impossible to deduce how recent. The parking spots were all empty anyway. One set of tracks looked fresher than the others, but how fresh, exactly, I couldn't tell. Besides, who would take off into this squall unless they had to?

Back at the room, I planted my ass on the doorstep, staring into a curtain of white. I extracted my new Marlboros, packing them against my wrist, a strictly amateur move. Didn't do a damn thing. Force of habit. I peeled the cellophane wrapper, struck a match. What a night.

"Got an extra one of those?"

She was young, early twenties, maybe. But haggard as hell. Skin puckered and parched as a Dust Bowl mother. She might've been pretty at one time, but it was obvious that time was long gone. And it was just as clear where she'd lost it.

The girl leaned inside the frame next door, hooded sweatshirt pulled over a tattered, twisted skirt, sedated eyelids and noodle legs fighting to stay up. I thought she might pass out just from standing there.

I hoisted myself and offered her the flipped-open pack. She reached out apprehensively, carefully considering her options, as though some future happiness hinged on making the correct choice.

I cupped a match and lit it for her.

She struck a seductive pose. Or, rather, she approximated what she thought one looked like from watching movies and TV, arching her back, arm crooked and draped above her head, knee up, sultry pout. The more I studied her, the younger I thought she might've been.

"Are you looking for something?" she asked, voice dropping to a throaty purr. Between her pale, skinny legs and dead, droopy eyes, there was nothing sexy going on.

"Actually, yes. I am. My friend."

"Oh," she said, and, realizing there was no chance for a sale, planted both bare feet on the cold concrete.

"Did you see anyone leave this room?" I asked.

She shrugged, then slinked back inside, leaving the door open, which I took as an invitation.

The girl plopped on the bed, Indian style, and grabbed the remote, flicking on the bulky set with the disinterest of a precocious seven-year-old child already bored by Saturday morning cartoons. A gray glow cast over her pallid features. I stood in the entranceway, unsure if I should fully commit, or just ask what I needed to know from where I stood. I didn't think I wanted to step into this girl's world.

"My friend called me from the room next door," I said. "About ten minutes ago. But he's not there now."

She glanced in my general direction. "Maybe he left," she said with a shrug. "You can come in. But close the door. It's cold."

Didn't have any other leads. I stepped inside and softly shut the door.

Poor television reception flickered like a strobe. If how Pete Naginis died had startled me, then how this girl lived was outright revolting. The room stank like foul, old sponge, and despite my work boots and two pairs of socks, the carpet squinched between my toes with a moist fungus. She made no effort to conceal her addiction. A pair of charred spoons and BIC lighters, cigarette filter, teeth-torn and balled for cotton, rested atop an end table a few feet away.

She set her lit cigarette right on the spread and tugged the sweat-shirt over her head. Plucked the smoke, swatted the ash, and fell back, reclining on elbows, bony breasts poking out. Her skirt hitched enough to reveal a stretched-out red thong that had probably been peeled more times than bulk potatoes in a soup kitchen.

She stared at me, and I got a good look into those dead eyes. In her own environment, I couldn't even put her at eighteen.

"What are you out in this mess for?" she finally asked.

"It's a long story," I said.

"You in a hurry?"

Good point. Besides, I couldn't leave Charlie stranded at the TC. He'd have to come back sooner or later.

"Sit down," she said, drawing on the cigarette, letting the long ash fall unheeded. "I won't bite."

I glanced over at the only place to sit beside the bed, the chair next to the drug station, giving it a quick once-over to make sure I wasn't going to jab my ass with a hypodermic.

I pointed through the wall, as if the pantomime would elicit the answer I wanted. "You sure you didn't hear anything next door? Anything at all?"

"I heard you calling for somebody. That's why I poked my head out." She held up the rapidly dissipating cigarette. "I was out."

I pulled out my cell to check if I'd missed any calls. I felt like a teenager making sure the phone still worked because my crush of the moment hadn't called back yet. Ridiculous. I'd feel it vibrate. I sent Charlie a quick text that I was next door, just in case.

"You don't know Chris Porter, by any chance, do you?" I knew it was a long shot.

"Sorry," she said, fidgeting with her legs, tugging her skirt down, all of a sudden acting self-conscious, or maybe simply cold, even though the radiator was jacked to a hundred.

"He's my brother. He's missing. He's a junkie. I was hoping maybe you'd seen him around the truck stop. I heard he spends a lot of time here. A friend of his told me. She said he goes with guys, y'know?"

"I get it," she said.

I don't know why I'd blurted confessions to an underage prostitute in an auto court motel in the middle of a snowstorm. Maybe I needed to talk to someone, since I had a billion thoughts squirming around in my head and no other way to let them out.

"Honestly," she said, "I wouldn't know if I had seen him. I make it a point not to get to know people around here. It's hard enough taking care of me."

I got it. Unless there was a chance to make some money, what was the point? Friendships with drug addicts equated to more mouths to feed. Everyone down here was a kitten in a cardboard box, an orphan begging for more.

"What's your name?" I asked.

"Does it matter?"

"No," I admitted. "Not really."

The girl stood and bent down, picked up an old fountain drink container at her feet and extinguished her cigarette stub. Apologetically, she asked for another. I passed her the pack. She considered her selection.

"Keep them," I said.

She didn't say thank you, just reached over me to snag the lighter from the table. I could see the inside of her arm, intersecting tracks from pit through crook to wrist, a down-bound train that ran all night long.

"That was his friend they found the other day," I said. "Dumped in the stream behind the store. He'd been strangled. Face busted up."

"Cops came around talking to everyone."

"What'd they want to know?"

"The usual. If anybody saw anything, heard anything, knew the guy."

"And?"

"Nobody sees anything around here." She attempted a smile. "I didn't know the guy. Like I said, I make it a point not to." She crossed her frail arm over her little boy body, twitching her legs again, knocking knees together, foot scratching calf, the jitters. "Not that it's gonna matter much soon. I'm not long for this place."

That might've sounded like a cry for help. But I knew it wasn't. Her wounds, whatever their roots, had scarred over thick, made her hard. This girl would survive. Which was the real tragedy.

"Are you moving?" I asked.

"Don't you keep up on your local politics?"

I didn't get the joke.

"They're tearing this place down," she said. "It's been all over the news. Putting up a ski resort or some shit."

"Must've missed it."

"Someone's about to make a fortune. They've been sending thugs around the last few weeks, trying to scare off everyone, clear the place out so no one tries to claim squatter's rights. Won't see *that* story on your evening news."

I remembered the soundless *News at Noon* report from the other day, the one where they interviewed the family on the slopes.

"What's the real story?"

"Overheard one of them," she said, "this tatted-up, muscle-bound dude, talking with Earl Hinkle—he's the guy that owns this place. Guess it's gonna be quite the resort. Fancy, five-star, huge."

I don't know what made me ask the next question, or why I thought she'd know the answer. But her response didn't surprise me.

"You know who's building this resort?

Her mouth twisted up. "That big construction company up here. What's the name? Lombardi."

* * *

Charlie still hadn't called when I walked through my apartment door just after midnight. I'd hung around the motor lodge and TC as long as I could, which was shortly after the junkie hooker, whose name I never did get, dropped the Lombardi bombshell. Roads would be closed soon. Had no choice but to head home.

It made sense that Lombardi would be handling the construction of a new ski resort, and the news alone probably wouldn't have registered at all, had Chris not broken into Gerry Lombardi's house a few hours earlier. If they were demolishing the motor lodge, I could only assume that meant the truck stop was out too. Surely, I would've heard something about that. Wouldn't I? Not sure a thread tied the two together, this new construction project and my brother's break-in, but the timing sure felt odd.

I tried to recall specifics from my conversation with Chris, when he'd been blustering about secrets and hard drives, and I knew the Lombardi name had come up in my talk with Turley, although that was hardly a smoking gun; my brother had had a problem with the entire Lombardi family since high school and the wrestling team snub, or at least what he'd perceived to be a snub. When it came to my brother, trying to separate fact from fiction was a sucker's bet and a loser's proposition. At the very least though, this Lombardi connection spelled a weird coincidence. Which made me recall what Fisher had said last night about coincidences: In the world of investigation, there's no such thing.

I phoned Turley. I knew he couldn't file a missing persons report on a guy gone only a few hours, but he could at least keep an eye on the street and an ear to the scanner. Turley said his shift was over but that he'd pass the information along to Ramon.

"What were you and Charlie doing out at the TC anyway?" Turley asked.

"Looking for my brother."

"Any luck?"

"Don't you think I would have led with that?"

"Too bad," said Turley. "I'd like to get McGreevy off my back. He's really taking this case personally."

"Isn't it a little strange that a Concord detective would be up here investigating the murder of a junkie?"

"He's not up here anymore," Turley said. "Headed back down to the city. Wants constant updates, though. Driving me crazy."

"I mean, why's the Concord PD so interested in Chris?"

"That truck stop has always been a lightning rod. Michael Lombardi's up for re-election in the state senate. His whole platform is pro-family and anti-drug. Won't help his campaign to have addicts fished from streams in his hometown. Plus, y'know, there's that whole business with those fancy new condos for the ski crowd. Don't want to scare off potential investors. Drug-related, violent crime sorta shatters the illusion of quaint country living."

"Speaking of which," I said, glossing over the fact that I'd just learned about this ski resort via an underage junkie prostitute in a motor lodge an hour ago. "I hear they reached a deal to tear the place down?"

"What's that?"

"The Maple Motor Inn."

"Oh, yeah, I think I read something about that."

"Isn't that what you're talking about? Replacing it with a new ski resort?"

"That'd have to be a pretty small resort!" Turley laughed. "No, I meant the new condos going up across town, big money trying to cash in on the Black Mountain crowd."

"I thought they were building a new resort at the TC."

"Not that I know of. Where'd you hear that?"

"I can't remember."

"The Maple isn't owned by the same folks as the truck stop. I don't know why anyone would want it, frankly. Kind of a dump."

"Maybe they want some new luxury condos there too."

"Next to the truck stop?" Turley said. "Who's plunking down good coin to live next to that freak show?"

"These other condos you're talking about—Lombardi's building them?"

"Of course. Who else?"

"You know who the developer is?"

"Don't recall. It was in yesterday's paper."

"That's all right," I said. I knew I still had the *Herald* lying around somewhere.

"Hold on," Turley said. "Got it right here." I heard rustling pages. "Um, it says the developer is Campfire Properties." He paused. "Why are you so interested, Jay? Looking for some investment property?" He laughed.

"Not exactly. I'll let you go. I should call it a day too. Just be sure Ramon calls me if he hears anything."

"Of course," said Turley. "I wouldn't worry too much if I was you. Charlie's a big boy. Probably picked up some sweet young thing at the Peachtree. So long as he didn't mack on the wrong trucker's girl, I'm sure he'll be fine."

I knew Turley was joking. But the comment got me thinking about that computer shop and Charlie pissing off those crazy bikers.

"Something wrong, Jay?"

Maybe it was time to trust Turley more. "Charlie and I stopped by that computer shop."

"When?" Turley asked.

"Couple days ago."

"And?"

"Have you actually been in there? Felt more like a motorcycle gang clubhouse than a computer removal store. Guys were tatted, jacked up, heads shaved, looked like they'd all done lengthy stints in NH Correctional."

"Commanderoes."

"Common what?"

"Commanderoes. Motorcycle club. Gang. Bad dudes. Not as big or well organized as the Hells Angels or anything, but still not guys you'd want to mess with."

"I thought you told me it was a computer shop?"

"It is. Your brother lives in a sketchy world. Attracts all sorts of un-desirable."

"Jesus Christ, Turley—and you sent me in there?"

"Hold on, Jay. I never told you to go anywhere. All I said was that Chris had a business operation. I never said to start investigating any crimes."

"No, just that it was in everybody's best interest if I found my brother first."

Typical cop doublespeak. This is why I could never trust them. It was a dirty cop trick. Technically, no, he hadn't told me to go up there. Just wound me up and pointed me in that direction.

"That stretch of the Turnpike isn't even in our jurisdiction," said Turley. "That's Longmont County. Gave them a ring after all this went down. Police Captain's the one who told me about the Commanderoes hanging out there. Probably trading hot merch for drugs."

"Stolen electronics? Drugs? Why don't you send somebody to arrest them?"

Turley laughed. But not like we were in on the joke together, more the way you'd laugh at a little kid who didn't yet understand gravity or the offsides rule in hockey. "Don't work like that," he said. "You need warrants, there's court orders, lawyers, wrongful arrest lawsuits. Protocol has to be followed. And, like I said, that's Longmont's territory, not Ashton's. It's not like there's a law against being high."

"Yes, Turley, there is. And laws against stealing and dealing drugs too."

"I don't know what they are or aren't doing in there, Jay. I'm only speculating. Nobody cares about a few dopers."

"Someone cared enough to send up a detective from Concord when one of them died."

"Yes, because it potentially affects careers and multi-million dollar real estate deals." Turley sighed. "If you want to know more about the Commanderoes, you really should talk to your ex's new boyfriend."

"Brody?"

"He ran with them back in the day, if I recall."

My stomach sank. I'd known Brody was in a motorcycle club. Just didn't think it was *that* kind of motorcycle club.

As if he could hear the panicked thoughts racing through my head, Turley did a quick about-face. "A long time ago. Like years and years. Sorry I said anything. I've been working too many hours straight. Should've kept my big mouth shut. You've got enough on your plate."

"What do you know about it, Turley?"

A fist pounded outside my door.

I automatically gripped the phone like a hammer.

"Open up! It's me, Charlie."

CHAPTER THIRTEEN

Charlie looked like a giant freeze pop, chunks of ice in his hair, skin tinged an unhealthy shade of blue, entire body convulsing with a teeth-chattering shiver as he cupped his hands and huffed into them.

"What the hell happened to you?

"Dude, you have no idea," Charlie answered, blowing past, searching my claustrophobic kitchen, scatterbrained.

"Did you walk here?"

"You have any beer?"

"Fridge," I said. "You sure you wouldn't rather have some hot coffee?"

He waved me off with a dismissive flick of the wrist.

I blasted the radiator, cranking the dial as high as it would go, old pipes sputtering before unleashing hot, hissing steam.

Charlie swiped a cold one from the top shelf, leaving behind the empty plastic rings beside the borderline edibles—a crusted wedge of Cracker Barrel cheddar, a questionable hardboiled egg at least two weeks old. He popped the tab and took a good long glug. A rosy glow returned to his cheeks. He dropped into the chair, kicking out his big, booted feet. Dirty snow water pooled underneath.

"Where did you run off to?" I asked. "You couldn't at least text me you were okay? I actually called Turley."

"Lost my phone."

"When? I'd talked to you, like, five minutes earlier."

"I ran into this guy who said he knew your brother."

"Where?"

"Coke machine at the motor lodge. Tweaker. Trucker cap, fuzzy little mustache. Never got his name." Charlie peered up. "You have any cigarettes?"

I reached for my coat on the table before remembering I'd given the whole pack to that girl at the Maple. "Sorry. All out."

"This kid swore he knew your brother, said he was supposed to meet him, in fact. That's when I phoned you." Charlie drained another swallow. "What'd Turley have to say?"

"A lot." I decided to hold off on motorcycle gangs and real estate deals for the time being. "So what happened? I take it you didn't find my brother?"

Charlie rolled his eyes and shook his head. "After I hung up with you, we're standing outside the door. Kid's jumpy as hell, flinching practically every time a snowflake lands. He's staring into the storm. A pair of headlights pulls into the gas station. Suddenly he says, 'We've got to go now.' And I'm, like, 'to meet Chris?' And he says, 'Yeah, Chris.' I told him I have to wait for my friend first. He says I can wait but he's leaving, and he takes off running toward that little parking lot—you know, not the main one, but the one for the motel."

I nodded.

"I thought, fuck, what if this is our best chance to find your brother? So I bolt into the blizzard, slipping and sliding, 'cause the snow's really coming down, and the tiny lot is up that hill. I'm barely able to catch up with him. I get in his car, this piece of shit from, like, 1984. Greasy, balled-up McDonald's bags, vending machine wrappers, scraps of scorched tinfoil on the floor, half of it eaten away by rust. I mean it, Jay. You could totally see the ground.

"Kid tears up the Turnpike. He's constantly checking his rearview, side view—like he's expecting someone to be behind us. He starts ranting about the DEA and other covert government organizations, how they're tailing him, tapping the phone lines, trying to scare him."

"Sounds like my brother."

"I know, right? But he's getting really worked up about it, all the time speeding faster and faster, and it's icy as hell out there. This kid is coming unhinged and we're about three seconds from careening off the Turnpike and joining that crane in Duncan Pond. I'm doing my best to calm him down. No use. He's talking about how the government's been sending agents to the motor lodge, roughing up everyone, slapping them around. I know he's high. I tell him it's all in his head, and that's when he reaches over and pulls up his sleeve. Welts and bruises, wrist to biceps. Like a goddamn eggplant, Jay."

I thought about that junkie girl telling me how thugs had been coming around lately, intimidating the riffraff to clear out the motor inn. These tenants didn't sign leases; you could kick them out with little due process. Then again, why bother? You could do whatever you wanted to these people. It's not like they were going to file a complaint with the police.

"We're tooling down the Turnpike," Charlie continued, "and he's pointing at everything—telephone poles, fire hydrants, goddamn icicles—and it's all some form of undercover surveillance. I went to call you and that's when I realized I'd lost my phone. Must've fallen out of my jacket when I ran to the car.

"We're driving through Ashton, and then we're out in the sticks, getting farther and farther from the center of town. I ask where we're going. He starts in about his wife he's gotta find, how she's the only one who's ever loved him and how he knows he fucked up, but he's gonna win her back and get it right this time, and it'll be like before, she'll see. I ask, 'What about Chris?' Kid stares over like he's seeing me for the first time. He doesn't even know what planet he's on, Jay, irises the size of nickels, and he's all, 'Who's Chris?'"

"Jesus, Charlie, what are you doing getting in a car with someone like that?"

"He swore he knew your brother."

With the heat blasted, Charlie had started to melt. I grabbed a towel from the bathroom shelf and tossed it to him to dry off.

"We ended up way out by that cemetery on 23," Charlie said. "You know, over by Eagle Ridge, before the 23 turns into the 12 on the way to Middlebury? The really old one with those crypts from the Civil War. He parks at the gate and kills the engine. I'm trying to talk sense into him, but really I'm thinking of ways I can wrestle away those keys. That's when he reached under his seat." Charlie panned over. "He had a gun, Jay. Put it right on his fucking lap."

"Jesus."

"Finger on the trigger, hand twitchy, he busts out sobbing—chest-heaving, snot-bubbling, like a little kid who can't catch his breath. Full-on waterworks."

"What'd you do?"

"What do you think I did? I got the fuck out of there."

"You walked all the way here from the 23?"

"Ran is more like it. Your place is before the Dubliner and a helluva lot closer than my house. I nearly froze to death."

"Had me worried sick, Charlie.

"Sorry, man. I knew you'd be worrying." Charlie kneaded the back of his neck, clearly frazzled over his midnight adventure. "I never knew this town was so fucked up. There's this whole world I didn't know about. That I don't *want* to know about."

I phoned Ashton PD and let them know Charlie was all right. I also mentioned the kid with the gun by the cemetery, not that I expected he'd still be there.

"You want me to give you a lift to your truck?"

"Mind if I crash on your couch and we grab it tomorrow?"

"Don't you have to be to work at like seven?"

"After tonight, I think I deserve a sick day, don't you?"

I pulled a pillow and blanket from the closet.

"Almost forgot," he said, peeling wet layers of clothing and setting them on the radiator to dry. "Got a call from Fisher before I lost my phone. Remember that whiny guy who called you wanting his computer back? The restricted number? Fisher did some digging. Goddamn pay phone on Archer and Black Spring."

I dropped the linens on the table. "Archer and Black Spring? By the old Armory?"

"Think so. Why? Mean anything?"

"I'm not sure."

"Who even uses pay phones anymore?"

I didn't say anything. But I knew the answer.

People who don't want to be identified.

* * *

I heard Charlie kicking around the kitchen in the morning and shouted where he could find that coffee I figured he'd be wanting by now. I rolled over and checked my cell. A little after eight. It was strange having so much time off work, waking up without an alarm, though I was hardly getting a vacation from all this.

We made a pit stop at Miller's for coffee and smokes. The storm had cleared and trucks were back out on the road. I filled Charlie in on my portion of last night. The junkie girl. The new condos and ski resort. The Commanderoes. Although in the gray light of a new day, I couldn't say the picture was any clearer.

The plan was to get some breakfast at the Olympic, where we could fuel up on coffee and pancakes, clear our minds, and try to brainstorm what the hell this new influx of information meant in the grand scheme of everything. That is, if it meant anything at all.

We were driving over to the Dubliner so he could pick up his truck, and had just pulled in the lot—dank fog descending the mountaintop like an inappropriate fairy tale—when we heard the sirens, and I saw the flashing lights in the rearview mirror. A squad car hopped the curb, screeching to a halt behind us.

Pat Sumner stepped out of his cruiser, donning his fancy, wide-peaked sheriff's hat, touching the brim like a cowboy on his way to church.

I unrolled my window and leaned out. Charlie, who had started toward his truck, stopped and turned around.

"Thought that was you, Jay," said Pat, cheerfully. "Good timing. Hi'ya, Charlie."

"How you doing, Pat?"

"You know what they say about complaining. Eighty percent of the people don't care, and the other twenty are glad it's happening to you and not them." Pat chuckled before shifting his gaze back to me. "Say, Jay, I need you to follow me."

"Where to?"

"Got a call this morning from Adam Lombardi. Seems someone hopped a fence and broke into his construction site last night." Pat let go a deep sigh. "Any guess who?"

"They sure it was Chris?" I asked.

"Video surveillance," said Pat. "Apparently, Lombardi's security has your brother climbing the wall like Spider-Man and mugging for the camera."

The relief I felt that Chris wasn't dead was instantly replaced by agitation. Mugging for security cameras? Here I was, freaking out and running ragged, and he was treating this goose chase he had me on like a joke.

"Why do you need me—isn't that a job for the cops?" After my brother had broken into his father's house and now his family business, I couldn't imagine Adam Lombardi would be itching to see me any more than I would him.

"Normally," Pat said, drawling his words. "Except Adam requested that I bring you along."

"He did?"

"Adam's a good guy. He doesn't want to press charges against your brother. Like the rest of us, he's concerned. We got to put a stop to this, Jay, or someone's going to get hurt. Real soon. Real bad."

I turned to Charlie. "Go home. I'll call you when we're done." Then added, quietly, "Why don't you give Fisher a buzz?"

"Okay," I said to Pat. "I'll meet you there. You got an address?"

"Yup. Site of the new condos they're building. Up by the old Armory. Archer and Black Spring."

CHAPTER FOURTEEN

Five portable trailers crowned the hilltop behind a tall, chain-link fence that walled in the construction zone like the borders of a miniature military city. Thick, intersecting black tubes ran from each trailer to a clump of bulky power generators that thrummed relentlessly at the middle of the site. Bobcats and bulldozers, perched at odd angles on the slopes, tore off tundra and ripped up roots, dumping mounds of frozen earth, stone, and wood into towering piles for other big, bucketed machines to scoop up and haul away.

The scope of activity was surprising, since I'd known plenty of guys who'd worked construction, and the chief knock against the gig was how work dried up in the winter. Not unlike estate clearing, the coldest months usually spelled layoffs, leaving employees scrambling to pay bills until the thaw of spring. Yet here was this site, kicking it in high gear. Appeared to be a massive project too. Must've been three dozen workers toiling about.

The wind kicked up as Pat and I trudged up the hillside. Loosened snow clods fell from evergreen branches arched high above the footpath and exploded at our feet, unleashing the pungent aroma of pine needles. For as aggravated as Turley could make me, I was sorry he hadn't made the trip. I found it easier talking to him than I did Pat. And I had more questions than ever.

Like we'd entered a war zone, felled trees and blasted shale spread outward in concentric waves from points of detonation, big bombs dropped from the sky. Not all was laid to waste, however; lingering traces of the man-made remained. Chewed-up sidewalk. Crumbled brownstone. Telephone lines threading the grove. Over the ridge, I spotted the shell of a pay phone booth. The Armory Building hadn't been functional in years; it was more a memento, a piece of history harkening back to the Revolutionary War. Didn't matter now. The Ashton landmark was gone—blown up, bulldozed, and buried to make way for some shiny new luxury condominiums.

Droves of soldier ants in hard hats scurried, lugging and lifting, toppling and tugging, shouting at one another in Spanish. Drilling jackhammers bore straight through the base of my brain, sneaking up behind my eyeballs, and kicking optic nerves with furious sonic force. The closer we drew, the louder, and more painful, it became.

Sturdy steel beams, sprung from the four corners, speared the leaden sky with statements of progress. Too late to turn back now.

Adam Lombardi—whom I probably hadn't seen in at least two and a half years, not since Jenny and I had run into him at Applebee's while she was still pregnant with Aiden—stood a grim field general amidst the rumble, barking orders at subordinates over the thunder and grind of retreating tanks. From that far away, I couldn't see his face, but I knew it was him. Like his brother Michael, Adam had always towered larger than life. Big fish. Little pond. Even when we were kids, he possessed a commanding presence.

As we approached the gate, Adam glanced from atop his mountain, then motioned for someone to go down and let us through, before turning and trudging toward a trailer.

A few moments later, a stocky, dark-skinned man swung open the gate, passing along foam earplugs and orange hard hats, gesturing for us to follow, as jackhammers continued their unyielding assault.

When we got to the office door, you could hear yelling inside, though, because of the elevated noise in the yard, obviously not the specifics. As soon as we entered, the shouting stopped. Adam, dressed in what I could only call blue-collar casual—tucked oxford, tan khakis—stood stern-faced and flush, looming over a college-age girl, who clutched a sheet of paper in trembling hands. Upon seeing us, Adam instantly changed tack, washing away all hostility, expression transforming into welcome and warmth. He politely dismissed the girl. When she walked past, I could see her eyes were red and rimmed with tears.

Once the door closed, the office was surprisingly quiet, considering the sonic battlefield we'd just navigated.

Noting my surprise at this, Adam pointed at the roof. "Sound-proofing," he said. "Had it done in all the trailers. Cost an arm and a leg, but worth every penny. Need to be able to get away and think." He smiled wide.

We all shook hands, and Adam made sure to look me in the eyes and say my name. The hello felt less organic and more calculated strategy, a sales tip he'd picked up from a Dale Carnegie workshop or one of those Landmark seminars.

You certainly got your fill of the Lombardi brothers growing up in Ashton. They were easily our greatest success story. They played the part well. Black hair, blue eyes, athletically built, with sharp, dark, Italian features. They sported the quintessential all-American look, and both possessed the genial, dignified manner of the self-assured. It occurred to me more than once that Michael and Adam could've swapped professions, and each would've been equally at home in the other's shoes.

"How's Jenny?" Adam asked. "Aiden?" The earnestness was palpable.

"They're okay."

"I was sorry to hear it didn't work out with you two." Adam acted a little uncomfortable when he said this, lips compressing into a tight, thin line. I couldn't help but feel this was also slightly staged, the way he momentarily cast his eyes askance, then knitted his brow, as though he too were mourning the loss of something precious.

Adam pointed down at his desk and a framed picture. It featured him and his wife, Heather, and their two sons, Adam Jr. and John, both boys dressed identically in green, collared golf shirts, posed in front of a wood-slat fence beneath a cherry tree against a powder blue background. The boys had inherited Adam's black hair and square jaw. "I know how rough it can be," he said. "I'd be lost without my family."

We waited while Adam gazed wistfully at the JCPenney family portrait.

It was Pat who finally broke the silence. "I suppose you'll want to be showing us that security tape?"

Adam smirked and unclipped the phone on his belt, tilting it sideways like a CB radio. "Luis, get me the surveillance disc from last night."

A voice clipped through the static.

A few minutes later, we were all gathered around a plasma TV while Adam hit "play" on the DVD player. A black and white recording with eight split screens popped up, last night's date and time stamped in military hours in the upper right-hand corner. Adam fast-forwarded until about the three a.m. mark, pointing at the lower left of the screen.

"There," he said.

You could see a hooded figure scaling the fence and dropping on the other side, zigzagging and darting in the shadows through falling snow, moving from box to box, working his way across the grid like the world's least graceful ninja. The figure, bundled in scraggly overcoat and bum gloves, morphed clearly into my brother.

In the last box, he's standing on the doorsteps, banging at the lock with a rock, when he abruptly looks up and realizes he's on camera. Instead of running off, my dipshit brother peers directly into the lens and smiles, displaying a mouthful of rotting teeth.

Adam clicked it off.

"That's your brother, all right," Pat said to me.

All I could do was nod.

"Anything missing?" Pat asked Adam.

Adam shook his head no, then pointed out the window to another trailer. "That's the one he tried breaking into. Set off the alarm. Central Security called me. I've got my own guys monitoring the site. They were on their meal break. Good thing, too. They aren't as easygoing as I am." Adam winced a grin. "When I got down here, I checked the tape and saw who it was." Adam shook his head solemnly, before making direct eye contact with me. "Decided we'd wait till the morning to call the police and get this sorted out."

"That was mighty white of you," Pat said, nudging me. "Don't you think, Jay?"

"Sure. Thanks."

Adam exhaled. "I honestly don't know what your brother's beef with me is, Jay. Been that way since we were on the wrestling team back in high school. You know, he always thought my dad screwed him out of his rightful place at the State Championships by selecting me because I was his son." He paused. "You have to believe me, if I'd have known that one single event would mess up his life so badly, I would've begged my father to take him instead of me." Adam tried to laugh. "We're going on twenty years. He can't really still be mad about a snub in high school, can he?"

"I don't try to guess what goes on in my brother's head," I said. I couldn't begin to fathom what this was all about. I didn't know why Chris was hopping fences into Adam Lombardi's construction site in the middle of the night, or why he was breaking into Gerry Lombardi's house. I didn't know what was really on that hard drive or who had killed Pete Naginis. If it was a drug deal, or trick turned bad, or what. But I agreed with Adam about one thing: None of this had jack shit to do with high school wrestling.

"Do you want to press charges?" Pat asked.

Adam paused thoughtfully, as if he were really weighing the option, then shook his head. "Of course not." He turned to me. "I'd like to see your brother get the help he needs," before adding the obligatory, "Let me know if there's anything I can do."

He reached out to shake our hands. When he caught my eyes this time, he stared harder.

"Let me walk you guys out," he said, pointing at the hard hats on the desk. "Don't forget those. Wouldn't want anyone getting hurt." Then he flashed those smooth politician, pearly whites again.

* * *

At the bottom of the hill, the grinding of construction faded into the valley wind. Adam bid Pat goodbye, walking with me to my truck. It became obvious he wanted to say something in private.

"Pretty impressive," I said, motioning toward the site. "Is this going to be part of the new resort?" Even though the motor lodge and truck stop were a few miles apart, and nothing formal had been announced, it was clear the two projects were related. Nobody was building condos on the edge of nowhere, and I didn't buy Turley's explanation that this was for Black Mountain to reap the reward. I wanted to deliver a jab that I knew he was up to something, even if I wasn't entirely sure what that something might be.

"You could say that," Adam responded, without surprise. "We're in the preliminary stages, but when the new resort goes up, we're banking on folks spending a lot of time up here and wanting to invest in a quality residence. The resort is going to attract a certain crowd."

"You mean people with money."

"Yes, Jay, people with money." He repeated the phrase with the slowed-down, slightly perturbed speech of an adult explaining to a child that sometimes the good guys don't win, or that life isn't always fair. "People with money like nice places to stay."

"Where's the resort going up, exactly?"

"The truck stop," he replied in the same transparent tone.

"I saw in the paper that the Maple Motor Inn was sold. I didn't realize the TC was also on the market."

Adam scarcely acknowledged the comment, looking around, which was pointless since there was obviously no one remotely within earshot.

"Listen, Jay," he said, tired of humoring me. "I need to talk to you about something. I'm hoping you can keep this private, between the two of us?"

I nodded.

"I wasn't entirely honest with Pat up there. He's sheriff of this town, and I didn't think he'd be willing to look the other way, even if I said I didn't want to press charges. But Chris did take something from me."

"What?"

Adam sighed impatiently. "I think we both know."

I didn't want to give anything away, but Adam was acting like there was nothing to hide.

He waited a moment until all warmth drained from his friendly all-American façade. What remained was cold, old-country mean. "You want to do it like that?" He didn't wait for an answer. "He took a computer that belongs to me. A hard drive." He made sure to enunciate every word. "I would very much like it back."

"I thought you said he didn't get in the trailer?"

A hard, fast wind kicked up ice and sand and spat them back in my face. I tried to remain steadfast and not blink, hold my ground in whatever this showdown was turning into.

"I'm doing you a solid," Adam said. "Giving you the chance to make this right before shit escalates and my security guys get involved. You don't want that. Trust me. I know Chris told you all about it, and I *also* know you and Charlie Finn went up to that old Chinese restaurant asking about it. So, please, Jay, stop wasting my time. Because this isn't a game. This is my business."

I pulled out my cigarettes, lit one against the elements. I hadn't expected Adam to be so forthright, and it was throwing me off. I had all these loose threads in my head that I'd been trying to tie together, and here he was saying, "Give me that," and handing me back the entire package wrapped in a nice, tidy bow.

"Sure," I admitted, "he told me someone had dropped off a hard drive at the shop he ran with his buddy, Pete—you know, the guy they just found dead—and that there was something . . . incriminating . . . on it. But he never said he got it from you." Which was true. I'd only figured out this morning that the computer might've come from Lombardi when I found out about the pay phone location. And even then, I couldn't be sure. I thought I had deduced a secret. I'd even paused over the word "incriminating" to see how Adam might react. But if my innuendo had registered, Adam showed nothing. His steely eyes remained unchanged.

Adam turned back to the trailer, casually. "That girl you saw me talking to? That's Nicole. Takes classes at White Mountain Community. Just started working for me as an office assistant, part-time. Nice tits. Dumb as a stump. Been here two days and already has misplaced a purchase order and screwed up my lunch. She's only working for me because I had to fire the last guy who did her job, Darren." Adam swept his arm over the breadth of his impending kingdom. "We're expanding.

This new resort is going to be a real boon for Lombardi. So I figured it was time we upgraded our computer system.

"I put Darren in charge of disposing of the old ones. And the faggot fucked up." This time it was Adam's turn to linger over a word. He said "faggot" with extra venom. Learning what I had about my brother's alleged prostitution, I don't think I kept as convincing a poker face. "I told Darren to toss the old computers, and I was explicit that they be recycled. Which he did, bringing them to a high-tech waste company down in Concord. Unfortunately, he'd forgotten a hard drive on his backseat, and, rather than drive all the way back on his day off, he decided that a homemade shop run by a bunch of tweakers on the Turnpike would suffice." Adam spat a gob of yellow into the white snow. "Obviously, he was wrong."

I couldn't understand why Adam was telling me all this. If Chris had been right about damning digital evidence of malfeasance, why would Lombardi be copping to everything? And then I caught myself. *Of course,* Chris hadn't been right about any conspiracy. How was this any different than the time he thought he'd been infested with botflies and poked holes in his forearm with a steak knife? Or when he was convinced that Dr. Johnson had put tracking chips in his molars? Even though I should've known better, I'd allowed myself to get sucked up into his drama, yet again. Standing there in front of Adam, I felt like a goddamn fool for trying to play hardball and subtly implying I was hip to some crime. Like so many supposed mysteries in this life, the answer had been right in front of me. My brother, who was always one bad hit from donning an aluminum foil helmet to stop the aliens from stealing his thoughts, had constructed a far-fetched scenario, and for the last three days I'd been acting a part in his fantasy.

"Having that hard drive floating around Ashton," Adam said, "in some junkie's hands, is bad for business. It contains intimate, professional details of all the transactions we've brokered with vendors, providers, associates—going back ten, twelve years. There are financial records, bank statements, on that thing. It makes my company look extremely *un*professional, paints the Lombardi name in a bad light. If our clients find out we've been so careless with their trust and private information, the company I've built from the ground up—that I use to put food on my family's table—will be done irreparable harm. I'm sure you can appreciate that."

"I don't know what you want me to do," I said. "I don't know where my brother is, and not for lack of looking. Charlie and I spent a wild, crazy night down at the TC yesterday. That videotape you played, that's the first I've seen Chris since I let him crash at my place three nights ago. He hasn't called. He hasn't stopped by. Hasn't written a note. My apartment was broken into, my head got whacked good, and—"

Adam had stopped listening, like my reportage was yesterday's news. He exhaled with exasperation.

I saw a Lombardi work truck round the corner, creeping toward us.

"Like I told Turley and Pat, if Chris contacts me, I'll let you guys know. Believe me, I don't want my brother considered a murder suspect. I know he had nothing to do with Pete Naginis' death. As long as he's running around, he's putting himself in danger. We're all on the same side here."

Adam slapped on that politician's grin, reaching out and giving my shoulder a tight squeeze. "Glad to hear it," he said.

The Lombardi truck, a giant, gas-guzzling 4x4, rumbled to rest at the curb.

"Thanks for coming down, Jay," Adam said, extending a hand.

Which I took, embarrassed for participating in the cloak and dagger bullshit of the past few days. Adam Lombardi didn't give a damn about preserving Ashton's history or its small-town roots. I knew he only cared about making money, no matter how many armories or motels he had to destroy to make it. But that was business. Lost in all this was that my brother, perpetual screw-up that he was, actually had a job to do too. Instead of simply erasing a hard drive like he advertised and had been paid for, he betrayed a trust, getting gacked on crank, snooping, then making up elaborate lies, and now those lies threatened someone else's livelihood. Add to that breaking and entering? No wonder Adam was pissed and losing patience.

I heard the truck door slam shut and heavy work boots approaching on the hard snow. Shaking my head in disbelief over my gullibility, I looked up.

"Jay, this is Erik. He's head of my security."

I stared at the jacked biker with the shaved head and Star of David tattooed on his neck.

CHAPTER FIFTEEN

"Are you sure it was him?" Charlie asked.

"How many other guys around here are built like brick shithouses with the Star of David tattooed on their goddamn neck?"

"Did he recognize you?"

"If he did, he didn't show it."

After Adam introduced us, Bowman, or Erik, whatever the fuck his name was, barely acknowledged my presence, and the two soon turned and walked away, leaving me standing in the cold with my head spinning. I felt like I was going backwards on an upside-down roller-coaster. I didn't know what to think, except I was getting sick of trying to figure it out. I longed to be back at some dead guy's house, where the only problems that needed sorting were packed away in the attic.

The pretty Greek waitress brought us our breakfasts: chicken-apple sausage, cheddar and mushroom omelets, hash browns, pancakes, buttered rye toast. And a basket of chicken wings for Charlie, extra sauce. I was famished. I smiled politely as she refilled our coffees. I couldn't tell if it was the same girl from the other day or just another in the endless parade of stunning daughters.

"So, Adam had those guys waiting at the shop for what? Chris to come back? You to come poking around?"

I tore open a fistful of sugar.

"It was probably one of them who clocked you over the head too."

"Or, maybe my brother told a fairy tale to some tweaker, who thought he could flip the golden goose for some quick cash. Who the fuck knows? But I'm done with it."

"Nah," Charlie said, "I'm putting my money on those bikers." You could see his gears turning. "But, wait, so they're not really bikers, then? I thought Turley told you they were in a gang or something?"

"Motorcycle club. The Commanderoes."

"Same as your girlfriend's boyfriend?"

"Jenny isn't my girlfriend anymore, Charlie, and if she was, then Brody couldn't be her boyfriend, could he?"

"You know what I mean." He poured a steady stream of half and half into his mug, swirling until his coffee was as light and sweet as melted coffee ice cream. "You think this Bowman—"

"Erik."

"You think this Erik had anything to do with Pete Naginis' murder?"

"I don't know." I slathered the flapjacks with butter, smothering my plate in a thick coat of syrup. "Guys like Pete live hard. Remember that hooker they found in the dumpster a couple summers ago?"

I hoped that explanation would suffice. Charlie, however, was just getting warmed up.

"How does McGreevy fit into all this? You think Michael Lombardi sent him up here? And if Erik Bowman *did* kill Pete, then the order came from who—Adam Lombardi? Whoa, man. That's huge!" Charlie paused. "But wait. What about the ski resort?"

I set down my fork. "I don't know, Charlie. Maybe Adam hired some ex-bikers because they're tough and construction is a tough racket. Maybe what Adam said is one hundred percent true, and someone dropped off a hard drive to be wiped clean and my brother and his druggie pal went rooting around, saw numbers that didn't make sense, and decided to construct some elaborate scenario and cause a row. Then maybe Pete Naginis blew the wrong trucker and got his neck snapped. How the fuck should I know?"

"And the sale of the motor inn." Charlie tapped his head. "Very strange timing."

"A coincidence."

"You know what Fisher said about—"

"Fuck what Fisher said!"

"Jesus. Take it easy." Charlie motioned with both hands to keep it down.

I had been talking pretty loudly.

Charlie waited a moment. "You have to admit, there are a lot of unanswered questions. Like why would someone looking to build a sprawling ski resort buy up a little motel first and not the truck stop next door, which is, like, twenty times as big?"

I shrugged.

"And none of this tells us why Chris broke into Mr. Lombardi's house. Or what he was doing trespassing at the construction site. Plus, you never answered why a detective from Concord is up investiga—"

"Because my brother is a paranoid, whack-job drug addict?" I could feel myself starting to grind my molars the way I did every time I got riled. "I don't know why McGreevy is on the case or why Adam Lombardi has a bunch of ex-bikers working security detail. But everyone needs a job, right? You keep trying to make a mystery out of this, Charlie, but the only mystery is how I got duped into running around Ashton playing Sherlock Holmes. There is no mystery. There is no big secret. My brother got his grubby hands on something he shouldn't have, and now he's driving Adam Lombardi nuts. Same way he drives everyone nuts if you give him enough time. End of story."

"Fine. But then who hit you over—"

I slammed my fist down on the table, causing the other customers and the pretty Greek waitress to whiplash and stare.

I held up my hands, smiling to let strangers know they weren't in the diner with a madman.

"Christ," Charlie said, as though I'd hurt his feelings. "I'm only trying to help."

"I'm done playing this game. I don't know where my brother is or what he's doing. Let the cops find him and figure it out. That's their job. Not mine."

Charlie grew real silent. Nobody said anything for a long time. I flipped through the jukebox for something to do. I'd hated '80s music the first time around. Charlie poked around his wings, not eating any. Tractor-trailers barreled along the boulevard, the thrum of a thousand oily gears clicking in place, faceless drivers tearing through this town on their way to somewhere better.

"You don't think your brother could've killed Pete, do you?" Charlie asked.

I wasn't sure what had gotten me so worked up, since Charlie had only been voicing the same concerns I had. Until he asked me that question, and I honestly considered my answer.

"I don't know," I said.

The diner's front doorbell dinged, and I peered past Charlie's shoulder, down the long tin corridor and over the black and white tiles pooled with muddy, melted snow to where Fisher stood.

"What's he doing here?"

"You told me to call him," Charlie said. "Before you went to Lombardi's. Remember?"

"Yeah, but I didn't—"

"Boys," said Fisher, reaching over the table and snaring a piece of toast from my plate. He crammed it in his mouth, whole, dropping into the seat next to Charlie. "You mind?" he asked, pointing at my food. He didn't wait for a response before he started helping himself.

Fisher extracted a manila folder from inside his winter coat and slapped it down, like a hot hand at the poker table. He craned around toward the door. "Can I get some coffee?" he called to the pretty Greek waitress, who was restocking muffins under a plastic lid at the opposite end.

Fisher panned from Charlie to me, then back to Charlie. "Who died?"

"Jay's lost faith in the cause," Charlie said.

"There *is* no cause," I said.

Fisher double-tapped the folder. "This might restore some religion."

"What's that?" I asked.

Fisher picked a rye seed from his teeth. "What would you say if I told you that Lombardi just landed a new, big-money contract?"

The waitress arrived with a fresh pot of coffee and poured Fisher a steaming cup. He attempted a look. She pretended not to notice.

"I'd say, 'No shit?' The motor lodge sale has been all over the news, and I was just at the site of the new condos, where Adam Lombardi was talking freely about the proposed resort, like it's a foregone conclusion and not some well-kept secret. Nothing to see here. Move along."

"Ski resort and condos," Fisher continued, as though I hadn't said anything. He picked through the basket of bones. "We're talking millions to the construction company that wins the bidding."

"I know all about it," I said. "I was up at the site." I didn't see why I needed to repeat myself.

"Okay, smart guy," said Fisher, twirling a plump wing in my face. "But did you know that the company awarding the contract, Campfire Properties, is located out of Concord, and that one of the members on its board of directors is—"

"Michael Lombardi," answered Charlie, who was already thumbing through Fisher's report, acting smugly vindicated.

"Is there any law against one brother throwing business another brother's way?" I said.

"Actually, yes," replied Fisher. "When it's a state or federal contract, there's a bidding process companies have to go through. To avoid collusion."

"The TC is privately owned," I said.

"The TC is," said Fisher, "but not the land it's on; that belongs to the state. They've been leasing it to the Travel Center. That lease is up this year. In a couple months, in fact."

Which made sense why there'd been an announcement for the Maple Motor Inn but nothing on the bigger truck stop. There was no acquisition needed. If what Fisher said was true, state bureaucrats simply wouldn't renew the lease, allowing Lombardi and Campfire to wrangle control. Wouldn't be the first time two allies with vested interests brokered a secret deal behind closed doors.

Charlie fell back, throwing open his arms, like we'd just unearthed the missing strand of cosmic DNA that would tie together the origins of the universe.

"Don't you see?" Charlie said. "The hard drive!"

"What about it?" I replied.

"This must be what they found," Charlie said. "A digital trail connecting Adam and Michael. I knew Adam was full of shit when he told you why he wanted that computer back. Client financial records? Michael Lombardi isn't sending detectives six counties over because of a bank statement. Adam's not hiring ex-bikers to raid your apartment and beat you up for a bill of lading. Biggest construction deal in the state? A state senator just giving his brother the contract? This is *huge!*"

"You don't know that's what happened," I said.

"C'mon, Jay," said Charlie. "I get playing devil's advocate. I know Chris drives you nuts and that you are seriously pissed at him right now. But this—" Charlie pointed down at the folder. "This goes beyond your brother. This is the kind of money people kill for."

"It's a stretch."

"No," said Fisher, "it's illegal."

"We need to find that hard drive," said Charlie. "Turley told you that Chris was ranting about Lombardi when he went down to the station, right?"

"You know my brother's beef with the Lombardis. Been that way since senior year. And he was high as a kite that night, paranoid, delusional. As usual."

"Maybe he had a reason to be paranoid this time," Fisher said, flipping open the folder and sifting through. "Anytime a contract this big gets decided, it's by blind submission. So as not to curry any favor. To stop things like a friend giving a contract to a friend."

"Or a brother to a brother," Charlie added, his righteous gaze burning a hole through me.

"Contracts get awarded to the lowest bidder," Fisher continued. "There's protocol. Nobody's supposed to know another company's bid. If they did know, it'd be easy to come in low."

"Like *The Price Is Right*," said Charlie. "Y'know, when someone bids $800 on a washer and dryer and the next guy goes with $799."

"I get how it works, Charlie."

Fisher leafed through data he'd compiled. "Got dozens of bids in here. Contractors from all over New England. It's that lucrative a job. Wanna guess whose bid came in last?"

"How'd you get all this?" I asked Fisher.

"It's what I do, Jay. We provide insurance to half these companies."

I pointed at the folder. "Answer me one thing, Fisher—Anything in there prove Lombardi had prior knowledge of another company's bid?"

Fisher didn't answer.

"Didn't think so. Lombardi is the biggest construction outfit up here. It makes sense they'd land the job."

"Still need to submit a proper bid," Fisher said. "And be sure it comes in lower than all the others. No way to guarantee that."

"Adam's been doing this a long time," I said. "I'm sure he knows how to manipulate numbers to land a job."

"Why are you being so difficult?" Charlie asked. "Since when did you join the Adam Lombardi fan club? You were as freaked out by those bikers as I was. Someone sucker punched you in your own apartment. Pete Naginis is dead. You brother is still missing."

"No, he's not missing," I said. "He was starring in a Lombardi Construction security video last night."

"You saw these tapes?" Fisher asked.

"Yes."

"Had the date and time stamped in the corner?"

"Yes. This morning. 2:48 a.m. I remember exactly."

Fisher thumbed through pages, settling on a telephone log. "You see that call?"

I stared down at a local number I didn't recognize, calling another in Concord I didn't recognize. There were several calls between the two over the past several days.

Fisher pointed at today's date. "Last night. 2:57 a.m."

"So?"

"Don't you think it's weird that after Adam Lombardi's construction site is broken into in the middle of the night, the first number he calls isn't the police, but his brother?"

This time it was my turn not to answer.

"It's three in the morning, Jay."

"What'd you do? Get his phone records?"

"It's not hard to do," said Fisher.

"You don't know what they were talking about." It was all I had.

Charlie held up a finger in another "aha" moment. "We could find out. Don't forget, I work for the phone company. Be easy enough to tap the line."

"Listen to yourself. You've been working at the phone company for how long? You're going to"—I lowered my voice—"illegally tap Adam Lombardi's phone line? Forget losing your job, Charlie, you can go to jail." I stood up and pulled out my wallet, counting out bills, then gathered my coat.

"Where you going?" Charlie asked.

"To see my son." I took a final swig of cold coffee, exiting the booth and making for the door.

"If you see Brody," Charlie hollered down the aisle, "you might want to ask him about his Commanderoes buddies."

CHAPTER SIXTEEN

Cutting across town to Jenny's, I was praying that she and Aiden would be alone. Despite Charlie's parting shot, I had no desire to talk to Brody. Not about bikers. Or gangs. Or anything else. I only wanted to see my family. I knew Jenny's mom, Lynne, often watched Aiden during the day, but I didn't bother calling to check because I couldn't stomach the disappointment of the answer not coming back in my favor.

I didn't see Brody's truck in the duplex parking lot. It was a little after noon. His shift at the plant didn't start until three. Maybe he was grabbing lunch with a buddy, or picking up parts for his truck, or getting an early start. I didn't give a fuck. As long as he was gone. This was my family first.

"What are you doing here?" Jenny asked.

"I wanted to see my son."

"Um, sure," she said, taken aback by my unannounced visit. "Come in. I was about to put him down for his nap. He's in his bedroom. We were reading stories." She started toward the room, then stopped. "Would you like to read him one?"

I nodded.

Aiden's eyes lit up when he saw me. He shot up off the chair and ran over, and I bent down and scooped him up. I hugged him tight as I ever had.

After I read him a few stories, the last a long one about a talking chicken named Buck Buck who worked on the railroad, I tucked him in and gave him a kiss on his forehead, brushing his hair to the side. He seemed so happy to have his daddy there and when he started to fuss about me leaving, I told him that if he didn't cry, and went to sleep like a good boy, we'd go to the petting zoo in Crawford soon. I promised. I knew I made a lot of promises. But it was high time I started keeping them.

I quietly closed the door.

Not a peep.

* * *

"He was giving me fits before you got here," Jenny said. "He loves seeing you."

"Please. Don't make me feel worse."

"What's wrong?"

I shook my head. "I don't know."

I must've sounded particularly pathetic, because next thing I know, Jenny's got her arms around me, and, normally, I'm not the kind of guy to break down. I don't fall apart. You keep that shit bottled up, take your hits, keep moving. There's nothing worse than a grown man crying. Today was different. Maybe it was the stress of everything going on with Chris, or the warring going on inside of me, feelings intensified by having to drive to visit my own kid after refusing help from Charlie and Fisher at the diner. I didn't want to look into Lombardi and the ski resort, the construction contracts, and the murder, because I didn't want to give a shit anymore. Whatever finally broke me in that kitchen, I didn't fight it, I gave in, collapsing under the strain, and I let her hold me for a long time.

Jenny was so sweet—cradling my head against her breast, stroking my hair, my face, whispering that she was there and I didn't have to be alone—that I surrendered. In all our time together, I'd never once cried in front of Jenny. Not even when Aiden was born. I honestly couldn't remember the last time I had cried. I knew I had cried at my parents' funeral. But that long? Had I really not cried in almost twenty years? Apparently, I had a lot bottled up. I was sobbing.

Then something weird happened. Jenny started kissing my forehead, my cheeks, my nose, everywhere but my mouth. She kept doing it. Until I felt my arms wrap tighter, constrict around her, and then she's pushing me back toward the bedroom, and I realized I'm not crying anymore, and that the whole time we're doing this awkward dance, we've been peeling off each other's clothes, my skin hot, every inch of flesh burning like a bad fever about to break.

We fell back onto the bed, and she lay on top of me, and now she kissed my mouth. She kissed it deep, hard, our tongues wrapped around and probing, desperate hands groping, fumbling, searching, the click of buckles, the tear of cotton, and then her warm hand was on me, and that must've been the emotional release I needed because I was harder than I'd ever been. I could literally feel the blood racing, pulsing, throbbing; I was so hard it was painful. We kept our mouths smashed against each other, and I had my fingers inside her, slick like glistening sugar water, and then I was in her, and she pushed back on me deeper and deeper and deeper. It was like we couldn't get enough of each other, both trying to swallow the other whole, devour, possess entirely. Insatiable. We came together almost instantly, collapsing in exhausted heaps beside one another. I'd never experienced anything more natural in my entire life. Higher than any drug I'd ever taken, drunker than any booze I'd ever drunk.

* * *

Back in the kitchen, neither of us said anything, though I could see she had to work not to smile. And I did too. She asked if I wanted coffee. I mumbled okay. I didn't know what any of this meant, and I didn't want to ask. In that moment, I was back with my family, and that's all that mattered. And I knew something else: it's where I belonged. I silently begged that clock above the sink to stop. Don't let another minute go by. I didn't want to leave, or have one of us say the wrong thing, which would inevitably lead to a fight, because it always did. I didn't want this feeling to end.

Jenny waited with her back to me until the last of the coffee finished percolating and the timer beeped. She poured two mugs, grabbed some cream and sugar, brought it all to the table, and sat down. She did her best to keep a straight face, as did I, but neither of us could suppress it any longer, and then she turned away not to get caught, like we were a couple of teenage kids again. Jenny was biting her lip and I tried to catch her eye, but she wouldn't let me, turning her head more, and I kept following her, until she giggled and said to stop it.

Funny how one of the worst days of my life could quickly turn into one of the best.

I spooned sugar into my cup. "Where's Brody?"

"Down at the bank working out the loan details. Then he's going to work."

"He's not coming back?"

"Not till his shift ends, probably. Why?"

"I was thinking. When Aiden wakes up, why don't we take him down to the petting zoo in Crawford? He'd like that. My mom and dad used to take me there when I was little."

"It's closed, Jay," she said, rather coolly. "Closed down years ago. And even if it hadn't, it wouldn't be open in the winter."

"Oh." Hadn't thought about that. "How about, like, the Chuck E. Cheese in Pittsfield, then? It'll be fun. We could get a pizza and let him play in the ball pit. He likes pizza."

"What are you doing?"

"What do you mean?"

Jenny shot up and snatched my coffee, even though I hadn't taken a sip yet, and brought it to the sink. "You can't take me on a date, Jay. I'm not your girl anymore."

"I know," I said, "but we're still Aiden's parents, and . . . what about what happened in there?" I practically whispered it, though I don't know why.

"What about it?" she said, now as icy as last night's storm.

I pulled my cigarettes.

"You can't smoke in here. It's bad for Aiden."

"Why are you acting like this?"

"Like what?"

"All cold and distant. Five minutes ago, I was inside you, and now you're acting like . . ."

"Like what?"

Jenny's eyes narrowed, mean, the way they did before she unleashed a torrent, only she pulled up this time. She'd balled her little fists and was ready to let go on me. But she stopped. Christ, I'd never understand women.

"What's going on with you, Jay?" She said it so still and perfectly calm.

"With me? You're the one who jumped me back there, and now you're acting like you don't know me."

"I can't do this," she said.

"Do what?"

"This!" Jenny shook her head side to side, as if she had to work to keep the thoughts from getting too comfortable in there. "Nothing's different, Jay. That . . . was . . . nice."

"Nice?"

"Yes, but it doesn't change anything. My boyfriend is down at the mortgage broker's getting us a loan on a house, and we're going to move to Rutland, because that is what is best for my son. Just because you're all screwed up in the head over your brother and feeling lonely—"

"I'm not screwed up in the head over my brother— Okay. Maybe I am, a little bit. But not for the reasons you think. And I'm not saying these things because I'm lonely." I got up and moved toward her.

"Don't."

"Why? I want to be with you. I fucked up some shit, I know. Didn't give you everything I had, and I'm sorry, but I'll do better this time, Jenny."

I kept moving toward her, and she kept backing up.

"Stop," she said, now pressed against the counter. I tried to move in to kiss her again, but she wouldn't let me, kept turning her head, pushing me off. "I mean it, Jay."

"I know you still love me too."

"We have a child."

"Don't give me that. That's not how you still love me. You still love me like you did back there. Don't you think I felt it? You can't fake that."

"It doesn't matter if I do." She strained to push me away, but I didn't give an inch. "Stop it." She stared out the window, through the open blinds. "People can see in here. Please. Move."

I looked out the window. The streets were barren and white.

"No one can see anything."

"Let me go. I mean it."

I had begun to back off when a key turned in the tumbler and the door shoved open. The two of us froze like deer on the Turnpike, right before they get flattened by a big rig. Brody kept his hand on the door handle, mean mugging our way.

"What are you doing here?" Jenny asked.

Brody yanked the key out of the lock, glowering at me. He tossed his giant, clanking ring on the table. "I live here?" He made for the fridge, snagged a beer, and slammed the door. "What's he doing here?" Brody didn't turn to look at me as he asked. Using the countertop, he popped off the bottle top and chugged his beer.

Jenny spun around to the sink and ran the water. "Jay stopped by to see Aiden."

"That so," Brody said, slipping off his leather jacket, which, although faded and worn, was probably the nicest he owned. Underneath, he was wearing what he probably considered to be dress clothes, meaning not his usual jeans and T-shirt. He looked ridiculous in Dockers and motorcycle boots. Brody must've felt self-conscious, because he immediately tugged off the collared golf shirt, leaving only a wifebeater and torso covered in ink.

"I thought you were going to work from the bank," Jenny said, water still running, back still to him. "How'd it go, by the way?"

Brody smoldered by the fridge. He eyeballed me as he answered her question. "How'd it go? Fucking bank says we can't get a loan!"

I hadn't said a word since Brody had gotten home, and I didn't want to be there for this conversation.

"Give Aiden a kiss for me when he gets up," I said, and went to retrieve my coat from the back of the chair, but Brody hooked the chair with his foot, pulling it toward him, out of my reach.

"Don't leave on my account, Jay," Brody said. "Have a seat. I obviously interrupted something." He spread his arms in a magnanimous gesture, alternating his stare between Jenny and me. "Please, go on."

"Nothing left to talk about," I said.

"You sure? How goes the hunt for your faggot brother?"

"What'd you say?"

Brody pulled out his cigarettes, extracting one with his teeth.

"You know I don't want anyone smoking in here," Jenny said.

Brody lit up anyway. "Fucking bank says I can't buy a house. Better believe I'm smoking in the fucking apartment I rent."

Jenny slid open the window and a cold gust blew in.

"Yeah, Jenny was telling me about your faggot brother," Brody said. "Blowing dirty trucker dick down at the TC. That's gotta suck." Brody snickered. "No pun intended."

I lunged and snagged my coat. I could see where this was headed.

"Y'know, everyone in Ashton knows he killed your parents, that's been going around for years. But finding out your own brother, the one you used to look up to, is a whore as well?" Brody looked at Jenny. "I'll be glad when the cops pick up his sorry ass. I wouldn't want someone like that around *my* son."

"Okay, Brody," I said. "I get it. You're having a bad day. Sucks about the loan."

"What the fuck would you know about it, huh, junk man?"

"Brody, why don't you go to work?" Jenny pleaded.

"Why don't you shut the fuck up?" Brody said, swilling some more beer.

The open window chilled the apartment and the heater kicked on, a loud thrumming, droning beneath the floor.

We'd passed the point where I could walk out now. I sure as shit wasn't leaving Jenny and my son with this guy, not the way he was acting.

I dropped the coat. "I think I will stay."

"Terrific!" said Brody. "What do you want to talk about?"

"How about the Commanderoes?"

Brody set the beer on the counter and stepped up hard. "Excuse me?"

"The motorcycle gang you were in." I pointed at the big panther tattoo on his arm, the one that looked like a hastily done cover-up.

"That's their insignia, right?" It was easy to see how a flaming wing and a gun would fit underneath.

"You were smart to want to leave," he said, falling back, flicking his wrist. "Go back to hunting queers."

I could see Jenny begging me out the corner of my eye.

"The thing is," I said, "from what I know, those gangs—sorry, those 'clubs'—are for life, blood in, blood out. Can't quit. Unless you have some leverage."

"What's your point?"

"Nothing. Just, you must've seen some shit. There has to be a good reason why you were allowed to walk away."

We locked stares.

"Since you're so concerned about my brother's well-being, I thought maybe you'd want to help. Our practically being family and all."

I exchanged a quick glance with Jenny, who wasn't a fan of either of us at that moment, her eyes a seething mix of rage and disgust.

"Adam Lombardi—you know him, right?—seems he has some Commanderoes working security detail for him. I guess it's like a side business for them. Bullying tenants, strong-arming, breaking and entering. Now they're looking for Chris. You wouldn't know anything about that, would you?"

Brody got right in my face.

"All I know, *bro,* is if the Commanderoes are looking for your brother, you might as well arrange the funeral, because he's a fucking dead man."

There was no way around it now. We'd come too far. Neither of us could stand down. It was only a question of who'd throw the first punch.

There was a light knock at the door.

Brody and I stopped and turned as Jenny opened it.

And there stood my brother, bum overcoat draped over a Pac-Man T-shirt, hanging off his skeletal frame and stained with hobo filth; that goofy haircut looking even goofier in the light of day; his old, brown backpack slung over his shoulder like a Sweet Pickles kid about to catch the short bus. His dirty jeans sagged, but not because he was attempting any b-boy style; he was just so damn skinny.

Chris didn't say anything. And neither did anyone else. Just four misfits standing in the middle of a fucked-up situation.

I'd never been happier to see my brother in my life.

CHAPTER SEVENTEEN

It was Jenny who jolted out of shock first, taking my brother's hand and pulling him inside.

"How are you?" she asked.

He half flinched, half nodded.

"Sit down, Chris," she said. "Are you hungry? Do you want something to eat?"

"What do you have?"

"A sandwich?"

Chris nodded, moving between Brody and me, taking the seat I'd been offered. He slung his battered brown backpack on the table, gazing up at me.

"What's up, little brother?" he said.

Brody flexed once more, then retreated, resuming his position by the fridge, swilling his bottled beer.

"Want to grab me one of those?" Chris asked.

Brody toed open the refrigerator door, snared a beer, and flipped it to him.

Chris caught it, then held it up. "Need an opener, bro."

Brody didn't move.

"I'll get you one," Jenny said, opening a drawer next to Brody, fishing out an opener, and handing it to my brother. Then she opened the fridge and collected meats, cheese, bread, and mustard to make my brother a sandwich.

"Where have you been?" I asked him.

He motioned toward the door. "Standing out in the hall. Listening."

He turned back to Brody. "Appreciate you being so worried about me." Chris paused. "Sorry about the bank. Guess they decided you weren't worth the investment."

Chris was a drowned rat compared to Brody, who outweighed my brother by at least sixty pounds, but you wouldn't have known it from the way Chris talked.

"No, I mean, the last few days," I said.

"You know, around."

"Did you follow me here?"

Chris popped the top of his beer. "I wanted to talk to you. Can't use the phone. They're watching your apartment."

"Who?"

Chris rolled his eyes like I was every bit the clueless baby brother.

Jenny set the sandwich in front of him. She had even cut it in half. Such a mom thing to do.

"Thanks, Jenny," he said. "You're always nice to me."

"You're welcome, Chris. I'm glad you're all right."

Chris tore off a bite. "I wish you and my brother would just get married," he said through a mouthful. "Stop doing this dance."

Jenny looked around uneasily. "I care about your brother—the both of you—very much."

"No, I mean, Jay loves you. He's crazy about you. Always has been. Always will be. You're the only girl for him, Jenny. I've known my brother my whole life. He's never looked at another girl like he does you."

Chris casually looked over his shoulder, nodding in Brody's general direction, and wrinkled his nose disdainfully, like someone had just tried to douse a fart with air freshener. "It's none of my business, but you're wasting your time with that piece of shit."

What happened next was a split-second blur and a high-speed train wreck.

Brody leapt at my brother. In a flash, Chris, who had been sitting with his back to him, slipped out of the chair, sidestepped the bum-rush, and let Brody's momentum carry him past. He caught Brody on the flyby and smacked his head flush against the table. There was a sickening thwack. Jenny screamed. I tried to grab Chris, who pushed me away as Brody regained his footing and surged to pile-drive him back-wards, but my brother gave him the slip again, slithering around, sling-ing an arm over his neck, and choking him in a half-nelson. Chris deliv-ered a series of lightning-fast hooks to Brody's kidneys. Five, six, seven, just like that.

"Chris! Let him go!"

My brother did. For a second. Then he juked and refastened his hold under Brody's arm. I don't know how it was possible, given the size disparity, but Chris lifted the bigger man high off the ground, then body-slammed him to the floor. I heard Brody's arm crack, like a twig for kindling. Brody clutched his elbow, which bent unnaturally in the opposite direction, bone piercing skin.

"Holy fuck," I muttered.

Brody writhed on the floor, rolling and howling. Chris hopped up, goofy smile back on his face as though nothing had happened. My brother had lost his mind, completely divorced from reality. Not that I didn't enjoy seeing Brody handed his ass like that. Whole fight lasted less than ten seconds. You wouldn't have believed it from the damage inflicted.

Jenny stood, mouth agape.

"You'd better call an ambulance," I said to her, giving her a little shake, before whispering something in her ear.

I turned to my brother.

"Come on, let's go," I said.

"Sorry, Jenny." Chris grabbed the rest of his sandwich. "Good see-ing you. Thanks for lunch."

* * *

"Where're we going?" Chris asked, as I steered my Chevy beneath the trestles. "Don't take me back to your place. They're watching it. I'll jump out of this truck right fucking now if you even try it."

"Don't worry," I said. "We're not going back to my place."

Chris nodded, snaking skeletal fingers through strips of peroxide. He fervently scratched the sheared side of his head, unscabbing little bleedy bumps. "I have to talk to you, little brother."

"All right," I said, calmly, exiting the small town center and making for Lamentation Mountain. "Take a deep breath. You're safe, all right? I want you to relax."

"Where're you taking me?"

"Just relax. We're going up to Lamentation. Nice and secluded. Safe from prying eyes. We'll go up to the watershed, out of harm's way, and then you can tell me whatever it is you need to tell me."

Chris nodded. "You got a smoke?"

I took one for me and passed him my pack.

Clouds of fog rolled over the mountaintop, billowing down the sides like dry ice at a rock concert. He kept checking the mirrors.

"No one is following us," I said. "Now, you want to tell me what's going on with you? You broke the fucking guy's arm! I'd be surprised if you didn't give him a concussion too."

"Brody's a dick."

"That's beside the point. There are laws. You can't assault someone like that."

"Really?" He snickered. "Because it sounded like you were getting ready to before I showed up."

"Sure. I might've taken a swing. One punch. Chris, you sent a man to the ER."

Which was why I felt all right leaving Jenny and Aiden alone back there: the only way Brody was getting off the ground was onto a gurney. The smartest thing for me to do right now was to get my brother out in the open, where this mess could be resolved, peacefully, with no one else getting hurt.

Chris brushed me off.

"And don't be saying that shit to Jenny."

"What? That you're still nuts about her? Dude, that's the least-kept secret in town."

"Never mind my love life, Chris." I dragged on my smoke, stealing glances in my rearview mirror. I was getting as bad as my brother. "You know about Pete?"

"Of course."

"Do you know who did it?"

He wouldn't answer.

"Chris?"

"Maybe," he said. "Yeah."

"Now isn't the time to play games, Chris. I want you to get the story straight in your head, because in a few minutes, you're going to have to explain yourself. Understand?"

I took Ragged Pass, my old Chevy trudging up the snow-covered mountain, jostling along shifted plates of unpaved road. I veered onto the southern rim of Echo Lake before the bridge and drove to the water's edge. I punched the truck in park.

"Start talking."

Chris slung the backpack onto his lap and unzipped the front pouch. He dug around inside, retrieving a CD in a white sleeve. "I need you to take this," he said.

"What is it?"

"It's why Pete died. I need you to promise that, if something happens, you'll take care of this for me."

"What's on there?"

"Contents of a computer. Hard drive. Transferred to disc." My brother stuffed the disc back in the pouch. "Here take the whole damn thing," he said, thrusting the backpack at me. "I don't need it anymore."

"Slow down," I said. "Tell me about this disc."

"Pete kept the original hard drive. It's why they killed him."

"Who?"

"Who do you think? Those asshole bikers working for Lombardi."

"And you know this, how? You saw them?"

"Didn't have to."

Hard winds whipped up snowy dust, conspiring little tornadoes to dance across the frozen water.

"Do they know you have this?" I asked him.

"They're looking for me, aren't they?" Chris flung the backpack between us, covering his head in his hands.

"They're looking for you because you broke into people's private residences and vandalized property. This, *after* you and your friend took possession of something that didn't belong to you."

"That's not true. Someone dropped off the hard drive."

"Yeah, to have its memory erased, not probed and exploited. It doesn't matter. Adam wants it back."

"No shit, he wants it back! Why do you think Pete is dead? And now they want me dead too, because I know what's on there."

"What *is* on there?" I asked. "What is this damning piece of evidence you've been running around Ashton with? Burglarizing houses, setting off alarms at construction sites, driving everyone crazy. You've got cops all the way up from Concord looking for you. I don't know what you think is going on here, but it's hard to trust your version of anything these days. So whatever it is, you'd better come clean. I'm about the only friend you have right now."

Chris stared straight ahead, entranced by the swirling snow ballet.

"Is it information on the proposed ski resort? The construction bid? Campfire Properties, and Michael giving the contract to Adam?"

"Just take a look at the disc," he said. "Look at it before Adam finds it."

"Because if it is, I know all about it already. While you've been running around playing drugstore cowboy and Indians, I've had no choice but to dig into shit. And it might be creepy, and maybe even unethical, but greasing palms to land a construction job and proving someone broke the law takes a lot more—"

"It doesn't have anything to do with Lombardi Construction."

I stopped cold. "Wait. What?"

"It's not about Adam's company."

"It's not?"

Chris shook his head.

"Then what's on the disc?"

"Pictures."

"Pictures?"

"Of kids."

"Pictures. Of kids. This is why you're harassing Adam?"

"You're not listening, Jay. They're bad pictures. Little kids. Young boys. You following me yet? There's a man in the pictures. Doing stuff to them. It's fucked up."

"Who?"

"I don't know. I can't tell for sure. I mean, it's hard to tell. That's why I need you to look at them. The guy is obviously trying to keep his face obscured, but he's old. And fat and disgusting and hunched over and—I wish you'd just look at the disc."

"Not until you tell me who."

"I think it's Gerry Lombardi," Chris said. "I mean, it *is* Gerry Lombardi, Jay. Open the files. It's him. Go look at the disc, I'll meet you somewhere later."

"Mr. Lombardi?" I paused a second to let it all sink in. "Then this isn't about the ski resort or condos? Adam? Michael?"

"No! I mean, yes, I guess. Just not directly. The guy who dropped off the computer worked for Adam. He told us they were getting a new computer system at Lombardi. Since he only dropped off the one, I thought there might be others with more photos. When I didn't find anything at Gerry's house, I broke into the construction site to search for more files, pics, to download them onto a flash drive, get more evidence, have a better look."

"So you're not even sure if—"

"I'm sure! But no one is going believe a fucking thing I say. You know that. You don't even believe me, and you're my fucking brother! You think the cops are listening to a lowlife junkie? All I have is a downloaded copy. There's nothing linking anything to jack. I needed irrefutable, one hundred percent, ironclad proof."

"Jesus, Chris." I pulled my hands down my face, digging my fingers into my eyes, pressing so hard I made myself see spots. "Why do you care so much? I mean, it's horrible that little kids—"

"Why do I care?! How can you ask me that? Those are little boys! Not much older than Aiden. Getting raped! And some sick fuck is taking pictures, keeping them in, like, a digital scrapbook to get off on later—and you're asking me why I care?"

"Calm down. I didn't mean it like that."

"What did you mean it like, then? It's not my problem? Then whose problem is it? Who the hell is going to do anything about it? Nobody in this town, that's for sure. Nobody is going after the Lombardis.

They are fucking legends around here! They named the goddamn high school gym after Gerry Lombardi. He runs that charity so he can pick those kids off, one by one, with impunity. He's ruining lives! People will line up in Ashton to bend over backwards to cover this up, and you know it. And I'll tell you something else—if the computer came from the construction site, you can be sure Adam knows about it too. Michael as well. Why do you think they're pulling out all the stops to reel me in?"

"Hold on. You don't even know for sure—"

"I do know for sure! It's Gerry Lombardi! Fuck! Listen to me! Adam and Michael know about it! Pete and I got in that huge fight because Pete was trying to blackmail Adam. I told him it was a stupid idea, that we needed to get more evidence, but he thought we could make some easy money. He contacted Adam and *told* him he had the hard drive. And a couple days later, he's dead. Figure it out! They know I have that disc—if Pete didn't 'fess up before they broke his neck, our crew at the shop would've sold me out—and they won't stop until I'm dead too. Why else would Adam care so much about a piece-of-shit old computer he threw away?"

"He says there's sensitive financial records on there."

"Bullshit! You think he stores his client's routing numbers on his computer? That's not how it works. If you weren't such a Luddite, Jay, you'd know that. Sensitive financial documents? He's fucking with you. You know who handles his security—the Commanderoes are no joke! You remember the Donatello Bakery murders? That was them. Three dead. Shot in the back of the head. Execution style. What the hell does Adam Lombardi need a security detail like that for? To keep trespassers from stealing two-by-fours?"

"I don't—"

"Yeah, that resort *is* going to be huge. And Michael's tough-on-drugs, pro-family horseshit campaign is big too. And both those things come crashing down if it's revealed their father is a pedophile." Chris grabbed my arm, making sure he had my rapt attention. "You're my brother. I know you think I'm a wasteoid fuckup. Maybe I am. But I'm telling you the truth about this, and I need you to trust me. If you've ever believed in me, Jay, please, trust me on this." He grabbed the back-pack and practically shoved it in my gut. "Please. I don't care what happens to me. Just look at the disc!"

"Okay," I said, checking the mirror, jerking the Chevy in reverse. "We need to get out of here."

But it was too late. I hadn't backed up an inch before the swirling reds and blues filled the cab; high-pitched sirens shattered the still country air, regret stabbing at my heart.

But it was the look my brother gave me when he realized I'd betrayed him that cut the deepest.

CHAPTER EIGHTEEN

With my brother tucked safely in the back of a cruiser, I took in the magnitude of what I'd done: four police vehicles, including the spanking new SUV, parked cockeyed on the rock; Otis, Ramon, and the rest of Ashton's finest, who'd been called on to bring down the big, bad felon, raising shotguns and hoisting bullhorns, milling about congratulatory following the successful bust. I'd sold out my own brother.

"Was all this really necessary?" I asked Turley.

They'd torn into the reserve like they were ready for a gunfight. But the showdown ended in a whimper.

Once Chris realized I'd turned him in, he lost the fight. He simply opened the door and placed his hands above his head. But he made sure to part with that final, searing gaze. It was the kind of look I'm sure haunted Judas for the rest of his days.

"It's a big deal," Turley said. He studied my pained expression. "That was smart having Jenny call us. No telling how ugly this could've gotten." He forced a smile. "Boy, your brother sure fucked up Brody. EMTs had to load him up with morphine just to move him to the ambulance."

"Chris had nothing to do with Pete Naginis' murder."

"Your brother's going to have a chance to tell his side of the story." Turley placed a sympathetic hand on my shoulder. "I promise. Naginis ran with a rough crowd, everyone knows that. Just gotta follow protocol here."

"What happens next?"

"We take him down to the station and talk to him until we get to the bottom of this." Turley playfully punched my shoulder in a show of brotherhood. Weird thing was, given the events of this past week, it didn't feel entirely misplaced. "You've come this far. Try and keep the faith."

"And what happens when Brody presses charges for assault?" As if Chris didn't have enough cards stacked.

"We'll cross that bridge when we come to it. I have a feeling what happened in Jenny's kitchen was some good ol' fashioned, big brother protection. Besides, Brody isn't the most upstanding guy in the community. Folks with pasts like his can usually be persuaded to be reasonable."

"Thanks, Turley."

I stared at the back of my brother's bad haircut through the rear window. He wouldn't turn around. I couldn't help but wonder if this was it: the final rotting of a relationship left to die on the vine long ago. I hadn't felt this empty inside since my parents died.

Pat Sumner tapped the roof of the squad car, and the lights switched on. The rest of the cops stopped backslapping and climbed into their vehicles, patrol units reversing and K-turning, as Pat ambled between spinning tires, making his way toward us.

"You did the right thing," Pat said, approaching with hand outstretched.

If I had really done the right thing, then why did it feel so lousy?

Through the glut of exiting taillights, I saw Lombardi's 4x4 work truck bumping over the rocky terrain, swerving from the access road for a quicker route.

"What's he doing here?" I asked.

"Adam was worried about your brother, and asked us to call when we caught him. Seemed the least we could do after all the trouble Chris has caused the Lombardi family."

At the sight of Adam and Bowman stepping out of the truck, I felt myself tense up.

Pat slapped me on the back and headed to greet them.

"Relax, Jay," Turley said. "The worst is over."

"You have to do me a favor. You don't let Adam Lombardi or that security goon of his anywhere near my brother."

Turley squinched his face. "What's up?"

"You promise me. I kept my end. I called you and gave you my brother. We can talk about this later, but when you get to the station, you have to give me your word that *that* guy," as I stabbed a finger at Bowman, "goes nowhere near him!"

"No one but the police will talk to your brother. You have my word."

Adam and Bowman marched over with Sheriff Sumner yipping at their heels like a puppy.

Adam Lombardi watched the police cars tool down the mountain with his prize, but Bowman kept his eyes peeled on me.

"Adam wanted to thank you personally, Jay," Pat said. "He knows how hard this must've been for you. Don't you, Adam?"

"Absolutely," said Adam, joining Bowman in a fierce gaze.

"It's for the best," continued Pat. "We can't have folks breaking into houses and job sites."

"No, we can't," I said.

Adam dropped the eyeballing, reversing tack, and slipping back into his man-of-the-people persona. "You eat yet, Jay? How about you let me take you to lunch? Carter's Steakhouse in Longmont is pretty good. Helluva rib eye. On me. We can even go to that diner you like so much, if you'd rather."

"That's all right, Adam. I'm not hungry."

"Come on," he urged. "We can catch up on what we were talking about yesterday."

"Chris didn't give me any hard drive," I said, point-blank.

Adam laughed uneasily.

"Hard drive?" repeated Pat.

"Turns out Chris did take something from Adam," I said. "Isn't that right, Adam?"

Adam was too slick to get thrown off his game with any curveball tossed by me. Instead, he dropped his head, humbly feigning a mea culpa. "Sorry, Pat. I should've told you the other day. I didn't want to say anything and get the guy in more trouble. But, yes, Chris came to be in possession of a hard drive of mine. Has a lot of private information on there."

"Wait a second," said Pat, slow on the uptake. "I thought you said Chris couldn't get in the trailer?"

Adam repeated the same story he'd told me, in the same contrite tone, with the same genial appeal to help him retrieve his missing property. Except, today, it rang phonier than that politico smile of his. And I wasn't buying a minute of it.

"—client finances, spreadsheets," Adam droned on, "numbers and figures that Chris, in his drug-addled state, might've misconstrued. As I was telling Jay, I had hoped we could resolve this discreetly." He made sure to catch my eye. "But I guess that's not possible anymore. Doesn't matter. As long as I get my property back."

"Do you know where this hard drive is now?" Pat asked me.

"Last I heard, Pete Naginis had it. We could ask him. Except he's dead."

Another halfhearted chuckle from Adam as Pat looked on confused, and Turley weighed the gravitas of the comment. Bowman looked like all he wanted was five minutes alone with me in a locked room.

"Either way," I said. "I don't have it. So don't send your motorcycle gang thugs into my apartment in the middle of the night to look for it again, okay?"

"Motorcycle gang?" Adam sneered. "You sound as delusional as your brother, Jay. You should catch some sleep." He cast a sidelong glance at Bowman. "Erik, was there a box you forgot to check on your application? Are you in a motorcycle gang?"

"Not that I know of. I have a Fat Boy. Some of my friends do too. Sometimes we take them out for rides together." Bowman faked being perplexed. "Is that what you think, Jay? That everyone who rides a motorcycle is in a gang? You might want to stop watching so much TV."

Pat laughed, but not because he got the joke. He didn't know what else to do. Turley kept shifting his gaze between us. My temple veins throbbed, the way they did whenever my blood boiled.

"You really look stressed," said Adam. "If you don't want to eat, how about you let me buy you a drink? Follow us down to that bar you and Charlie Finn like so much, the Dubliner. We'll get us a basket of chicken wings, have a beer."

"No thanks."

Adam and I remained fixed on one another. I was so pissed for getting jacked around that I hadn't noticed Bowman straying over to my truck, where he reached through the open driver's side window.

"This is your brother's, right?" Bowman asked, lifting up the battered backpack.

"Don't touch that!" I shouted. "It's not yours."

"I'm sure with the rash of break-ins and thefts," Adam said, "the police have already examined its contents." He addressed Pat. "Right?"

Sheepishly, Pat nudged Turley to retrieve the bag.

"What the hell are you doing, Pat?" I asked. "There's nothing in there but a bunch of my brother's junk. Old cassette tapes he can't even play, a toothbrush he doesn't use."

"Don't worry, Jay," said Pat. "It'll be down the station with your brother."

Turley relieved Bowman of the backpack, passing it to Pat.

"Look at the size of the thing," I said. "Does it really look like a hard drive could fit in there? You can feel it. Does it feel like a computer is inside?"

"Actually," said Adam, as Bowman rejoined him like a faithful guard dog, "I'm wondering if Chris might've made a copy of the drive."

I remembered the beat-up junkies at the computer shop. Or maybe Chris was right, and Pete had given him up before they killed him. Either way, Adam knew exactly what he was looking for.

"It would be a CD," Adam continued. "White sleeve. We could avoid wasting any more time if we took a look now."

"Don't you need a search warrant to do that?" I said.

"Not when a suspect is in custody," Adam responded politely. "Then again, I'm not a lawyer. Of course, the backpack *was* in *your* truck, Jay. I'm not sure if there's a legal loophole there. You could give us permission to look, save me the hassle of having to go all the way down to the precinct. What do you say? Be a pal?"

Pat and Turley turned to me, awaiting my answer.

"Do whatever the hell you want," I said. "But hurry up so I can go."

Pat crouched and unzipped the backpack, poking around, casting aside a rubber-banded Tupperware container and toothbrush that looked like it had been used to clean grout; pulling out an old pair of stained underwear, which he held at arm's length with forefinger and thumb, before quickly dropping them back in the bag.

"Check the front pouch," said Adam.

Pat gazed over at me. I shrugged, disgusted.

Opening the pouch, Pat rooted through tangled earbuds and AV cords, scraps of paper and cards, then pulled out the shiny disc in a white sleeve.

"I'll be damned," said Pat.

"I believe that's mine," said Adam, triumphantly, glancing at me as he reached out to pluck the CD from Pat's hand. He stopped. "If it's okay with you, Jay. I mean, it was in your truck."

"Take whatever you want," I said. "Am I free to go?"

"Of course," Pat said, creaking to his feet and passing me the backpack full of worthless junk as a consolation prize.

I'd only taken a few steps when Adam called out.

"Thanks for all your help, Jay."

* * *

I phoned Jenny. She was at the hospital with Brody. I wanted to clue her in on what had happened, but she said she couldn't really talk. It sounded as if there were a bunch of people around. I apologized and thanked her. She hung up. I couldn't expect much more. This wasn't the time.

Whatever had happened between us, I should've been flying high. Only I didn't have a moment to enjoy it. Too much stood in the way. The scene in the kitchen, Chris and the fight, my brother's revelation on Lamentation, and that last look he gave me. The showdown with Adam and Bowman. And, of course, the biggest deal of all, the disc.

I needed to find Charlie. I knew where he would be.

Anchored in his usual spot, he sat along the counter at the Dubliner, nursing a beer, basket of bones picked clean and spread before him like a secret burial ground.

I pulled up a stool.

He peered over, nodded.

"Sorry about earlier," I said.

"Don't sweat it. I probably got carried away. I hate working for the phone company. It's killing my soul. Got swept up in a mystery because it made my life feel important for a minute."

Rita looked down my way, and I held up two fingers.

"You weren't entirely wrong," I said. "I found Chris."

"Where?"

"Rather, he found me. Jenny's."

"Shit. How is he?"

"He broke Brody's arm."

Charlie pulled back.

"Brody pushed his buttons, and then it was like my brother was back in high school on the wrestling team. Bruce Lee shit." I shook my head, holding back a grin. "It was nuts. I mean, he fucked him up, Charlie. I never would've thought he still had it in him. Brody's in the ER."

"Couldn't have happened to a nicer guy."

Rita set down our beers.

Charlie hefted his. "I know you try to cut Brody slack, but he's a class-A dick, bro, and Jenny is only with him because you won't let her be with you."

"We had sex."

"Who?"

"Jenny and me."

"When?"

"This afternoon. After Aiden went down for a nap. Before Brody got home. It just sorta happened."

"You old dog," Charlie said, beaming. He furrowed his large forehead. "How was it?"

"Amazing. It felt . . . like home. When Chris showed up, he told Jenny I was still in love with her. Then he called Brody a piece of shit. Which is when Brody went after him."

"And Chris fucked him up."

"And Chris fucked him up."

Charlie took a swig. "So where is Muhammad Ali now?"

"Down at the station. I was worried about him and wanted him somewhere safe, so as we were leaving Jenny's place, I whispered for her to call Turley and Pat and tell them where we'd be." I let go a deep sigh.

"And now you're feeling like shit," said Charlie. "I could tell something was wrong by that hangdog expression when you strolled in." He elbowed me. "You did the right thing. If Chris had nothing to do with Pete Naginis' death, it's best to clear up this shit right now. He's left running around Ashton, who knows what could happen. Cops find him in the dark, he reaches for a comb in his waistband—"

"A comb?"

"You know what I mean. When temperatures rise, people get burned. I mean, they get shot and shit. Happens all the time." Charlie flung an arm around my shoulder. "Don't beat yourself up. I know you only did it because you love him."

The TV was showing the Bruins pre-game. They'd dug themselves a hole too deep to crawl out of. It was a lost season.

"What did you mean when you said I wasn't entirely wrong?" Charlie asked, fisting nuts.

"When I drove with Chris up the mountain—that's where I told Jenny to have the cops meet us; I knew he'd be too paranoid to go back to my place—he gave me something."

I pulled the disc from the back of my pants.

"Anything on there linking Adam and Michael to some top-secret government conspiracy?" Charlie mocked.

"Chris says there's pictures."

"Pictures?"

"Of kids. And an old man, doing bad things to them."

"Kiddie porn?"

"Chris says it's Gerry Lombardi."

Charlie did a double take. "Mr. Lombardi?"

"That's what Chris said. He was convinced. Said that's why he broke into his house and the job site. He was trying to find more computers. Get more evidence. Chris says that's the real reason they're after him, and that Adam and Michael know all about it. Since their big plans would be derailed if this went public, they're trying to kill him. Of course, my brother also thinks the fluoride in the drinking water is trying to kill him."

"You didn't turn the disc over to Pat and Turley when they picked him up?"

"Nope. But Adam and Bowman drove out to the lake looking for it. Adam kept trying to get me to go off with him. But when they were taking Chris into custody, I switched the discs, in case my brother was right."

"If you didn't already believe he was, you wouldn't have switched the discs."

Charlie had a point. It had happened so fast I didn't have time to think; I acted on instinct. I grabbed my CD collection and made the exchange.

"What's going to happen when Adam—"

"Pops in Bruce Springsteen & the E Street Band's *Live in New York City*? I don't know."

Charlie pulled out his wallet. "You take a look at that disc yet?"

"You know I don't have a computer."

"But I do." He slapped a pair of tens on the bar, draining the rest of his pint.

"Where's Fisher?" I asked.

"At his mother's."

"Tell him to meet us at your place. I'd like to get his take before I move on this."

"What's your plan if it is Mr. Lombardi?"

Good question.

I didn't have a clue.

CHAPTER NINETEEN

Waiting for Fisher to show, Charlie booted up his old computer in the back of the house, and I emptied the old brown rucksack onto the living room floor. My brother's world unfurled before me. I stared at a mess of clutter and crazy person junk, like when Ally Sheedy dumps her bag-lady purse in *The Breakfast Club,* a movie my brother and I watched so many times when we were kids, we could quote it, line for line, until the part where everybody starts crying a lot and it stops being funny.

His driver's license was in there, expired, of course, picture taken back when he was still handsome, his shaggy brown hair carefully parted at the side. Drug paraphernalia, neatly rubber-banded together in a small, rectangular Tupperware container, which Pat had been kind enough to overlook. Through the plastic lid, I could see a charred spoon, needle, torn cigarette filter, aluminum foil, lighter. There were scraps of paper with numbers scratched in ballpoint, and business cards for free food items if ten holes were punched. None of these cards had anywhere near ten holes punched. Pair of socks. Plus the smeared undies.

I heard the front door push open. "Yo, where's the party?"
"Back here," Charlie shouted.
I got to my feet and joined Fisher in the tiny office. Charlie clearly didn't need an office. I remembered when he put it together after his mom died. It was the only room he redecorated. It had been her sewing den. Back then, Charlie had a hundred business ideas he wanted to put in motion. All-terrain vehicle rentals. Mini-golf/bar. Now, a small

computer sat on a Furio wood desk next to an empty wire basket. Dust covered the keys. A blue screen fizzled.

"Sorry," Charlie said. "Desktop's a piece of shit."

"What's the deal?" asked Fisher.

"I need a new computer. This one takes forever to load."

"I mean the disc," Fisher said, looking at me. "Your brother thinks Mr. Lombardi's diddling kiddies? That is seriously fucked up."

"Here we go," said Charlie, clicking on a tiny desktop folder, which opened into several larger desktop folders, each labeled by long, alphanumeric sequences. Charlie selected the first one.

We waited. Nothing.

"Is it blank?"

"Hold on," said Charlie. "Just takes a min—"

"Whoa!" said Fisher.

I could've gone my whole life without having those images stuck in my head, and now that they were, I'd never be able to get them out. What kind of a sick fuck does that to a child?

The pictures were amateurish and grainy, but it was clear as day what was happening, the unholy tangle of flesh. You couldn't see faces too well, most photos were cropped above the neck. But that didn't diminish the horror. They were all young boys—chubby, skinny, somewhere in between—put in positions little boys should never be put in, doing things little boys should never be doing. No two boys ever appeared together. You could tell the man in the photos was old by the withering, wrinkled skin, the age spots, and sagging body parts. His face was carefully edited out. The photos must've been taken with a timer. Unless there was someone else in the room, which added a whole new dimension I didn't dare fathom. The background in each was gray, dark, completely nondescript, and, therefore, unidentifiable, your average basement. No furniture, not even a bed, just cold concrete with the occasional wood beam, a cheap carpet laid on the floor, like one you'd throw down for a dog.

"Try another folder," I said.

There were seven folders in all, each with about half a dozen pictures, different kid, same location, same elderly man with bad posture making a guest appearance. The age would be about right. Without see-ing a face, though, the perp's identity was impossible to nail down.

As much as none of us wanted to, we clicked on every image, thor-oughly examining them, moving from victim to victim, and feeling hor-rified all over again. All I could think of was Aiden, who was only a few years younger than these boys, and all the fathers who had no idea what was being done to their sons. As a parent, you strive to protect your kid, keep him from harm's way. It's instinctual, primal. If Chris was right and this was Lombardi, he'd used his charity as a cover to earn the trust of desperate parents, only to pick off their children when they were most vulnerable—which made him the worst kind of monster.

"There's nothing we can use here," Fisher said.

Sadly, I feared he was right.

Until we clicked on the last folder. A partial view of a face. Slightly out of focus, but maybe . . .

"Is it him?" Charlie asked.

We all leaned in and stared hard.

"That's Gerry Lombardi," Fisher said.

"I don't know," said Charlie.

"Try the next one," I said.

Another partial view of the man's face. Perhaps a bit more . . . We clicked through the rest. Nothing. Except the shame of frightened little boys.

"Go back," Fisher said. "That one there." He pointed at the screen. "That's Gerry Lombardi."

"It sure does look like him," Charlie said.

I stared at the old man in the picture. I had Charlie zoom in, blow up, but the more we tried to manipulate the photos, the blurrier they became, until they morphed into shapeless, unrecognizable blobs. There could be no definitive answer. My best tool was my gut.

"Jay? What do you think?"

"I think it's him." I pointed at the face. "The bushy gray eye-brows. The ratty buck teeth. Even in profile . . ." I moved my finger down the image. "Look there. The way he's humped over like that." Mr. Lombardi's posture was unique and beyond abysmal, like a sloth with scoliosis. I felt the rage surge. I thought of that day at the Little People's Playground. Lombardi didn't have any grandkids with him. Didn't strike me as odd at the time. He'd simply been strolling the grounds, trolling for new victims. All that bullshit about beauty and the joy of laughing little boys? Made me sick. Right out in the open. His MO was easy to deduce. I recalled his sympathetic pitch for me to enroll Aiden in UpStart, like he was only there to help. Taking advantage of parents, stealing childhoods. Chris had been right. Who would do a damn thing about it?

"Should we turn the disc over to the police?" Charlie asked.

Fisher groaned.

"What?" Charlie said. "I thought you agreed it was him?"

"It *is* him. I took gym with that dirty old pervert. You could see the way he looked at you when you were changing or in the shower. That's Gerry Lombardi." Fisher turned to me. "But all you have is that disc? Not the original hard drive?"

"Chris said Pete had the hard drive."

"And Pete's dead." Fisher shook his head. "I can see why your brother was trying to get more evidence. That disc alone won't cut it. There's no digital coding, no electronic thumbprint telling us where the photos originally came from. You can't connect it to anyone. I mean, unless some kid comes forward. Has anyone ever accused Mr. Lombardi of something like this?"

"Not that I know of," I said.

"Won't stick," said Fisher, shaking his head. "Couple grainy profiles? No way. That disc is useless."

"But the disc was burned off a Lombardi Construction hard drive," Charlie said. "Surely, that proves something."

"That disc could've been made in China for all we can prove."

"Turn it off," I told Charlie. I couldn't stomach those pictures any longer.

I walked out to the living room, Fisher and Charlie tagging behind. I fell into the floral print couch, wrapping my head in my hands.

"Brought your brother to the station?" Fisher asked.

"Yeah."

"What are they going to do with him?"

"Talk to him, I guess. He didn't kill Pete, I know that."

Fisher looked deeply concerned.

"What is it?" Charlie asked.

"Listen, guys, it doesn't matter if he killed Pete Naginis. They'll say he did. Jay, this real estate deal, this ski resort and condos, we're talking tens of millions. And Michael Lombardi's political career? If there is any hint their father is involved in something like this—"

"You said those pictures don't prove anything," said Charlie.

"You think the Lombardis are taking that chance? You don't hire the Commanderoes as your security if your goal is to play nice. Somebody killed Pete."

"Could've been a trick turned bad," I said.

"Sure. Or it could've been the Commanderoes."

"What do you propose we do?"

"I'd get down to the station and talk to Turley and Pat. Put the cards on the table."

"You said that we couldn't use that disc. I'm supposed to walk into the precinct and accuse Adam and Michael Lombardi, Ashton's favorite sons, of murder. With no evidence? They'll lock me up with my brother."

"The disc *is* useless," Fisher said. "But they don't know that. Or else they wouldn't have been hunting your brother so hard. He's easily disposed of. You gotta come up with a plan of action. Worst thing that could happen right now is they cut your brother loose. Once he's out of that jail cell and back on the street, he's an open target, a sitting duck."

"What if Adam plants another prisoner to shiv him or something?" Charlie said, sounding worried.

"This is Ashton, Charlie, not NYC," said Fisher. "You've watched too many cop shows."

"Besides," I said, "I made Turley promise no one but the police would be allowed near him."

"Oh, Rob Turley promised?" Fisher scoffed. "Never trust a cop."

"Fine," said Charlie, his feelings obviously hurt. "Then maybe they ship him down to Concord."

"Why would they ship him down to Concord?" Fisher snapped. "Don't be stupid. You gotta think, Charlie. Concord has no jurisdiction here."

"Oh, yeah," said Charlie, "then why would they send a big city detective up to Ashton to investigate?"

"What big city detective?" asked Fisher.

"Cop from Concord," I said. "Was up earlier in the week, headed back to the city."

"They sent a detective all the way up from Concord? You never told me that."

"Why would I tell you, Fisher? We've hung out twice in ten years. This is the most you've talked to me since I felt up Gina Rosinski in high school."

Fisher's eyes narrowed to slits. He quickly relaxed. Nice to see he was finally letting it go.

"Fair enough," he said. "But it's weird they'd put a Concord detective on the case. What I'm trying to understand is, why?"

"We thought so too," said Charlie.

"Figured the Lombardis have some pull," I said. "Especially Michael."

"Pull? Sure. He's a state senator. But he can't just pick up the phone and have the cops working for him. Doesn't work like that. And why Concord?"

"This McGreevy's a real bulldog too," I said.

Fisher's face drained of all color.

"What is it?" I asked.

"Did you say McGreevy? Wallace McGreevy?"

"Yeah. Actually, Wallace—"

"—David John McGreevy. Concord detective."

Charlie and I exchanged a glance.

"How'd you know that?" I said. "We never told you."

"And you're sure that was his name?" Fisher asked.

"Yes. I saw the badge. The initials anyway—D. J. When he came up with Turley and Pat after someone broke into my apartment. I remember thinking the name was odd. Y'know, because of the saying about not trusting a man with two first names. Real abrasive asshole too. Why? You know him?"

"Not personally."

"What then? You've heard of him? Is there something wrong with the guy?"

"Only if you think there's something wrong with a dead man investigating crimes. I don't know how to tell you guys this. But Detective Wallace David John McGreevy died two weeks ago."

CHAPTER TWENTY

Back in Charlie's office, huddled around the computer, Fisher pulled up an article from the *Concord Monitor* archives that ran two weeks earlier.

Charlie read aloud over my shoulder.

"'The body of Detective Wallace David John McGreevy was found in his home early Sunday morning, the victim of a gastrointestinal rupture.' Ouch."

"I only knew about it," Fisher said, "because my company holds the life insurance policy on the guy. Plus, it's not a name you forget."

"So you think someone is impersonating a dead cop?"

"Someone's walking around with his badge, ain't he?" Fisher gestured to a block of text at the bottom of the screen. "Read the last paragraph, Charlie."

"'There appears to have been no signs of forced entry, although the police are not ruling out foul play.'" Charlie waited. "Huh? Foul play?"

"That's the thing," said Fisher, "and why I remember the case. Dude suffered internal hemorrhaging. They found traces of glass in his stomach."

"Glass?"

"Like someone had shaved a light bulb, the ME said, put it in his cornflakes or coffee, perforated his abdominal wall—fucker bled out. Nobody can prove it wasn't an accident. As if anyone eats glass by mistake. But he wasn't married. No girlfriend, no kids, lived alone. As a cop, you always make enemies, but with no motive or suspects, we'll probably have to pay out on the policy. Sister is the beneficiary. Lives in Kansas. Hadn't spoken to her brother in twenty-five years. Was shocked when we called her. Piddly policy. Fifty grand. Still, you don't forget circumstances like that."

"You can't just walk into the police department with a fake badge," Charlie said. "Can you?"

"In Ashton?" I said. "Pat Sumner is about a week from retirement. I don't think that kid Ramon speaks more than ten words of English. Otis? Turley? Really?"

We all looked at each other, thinking the same thing.

I checked my cell. No service. "Where's your landline, Charlie?"

He pointed toward the kitchen. I ran through the living room and found the cordless on the stove, and hurriedly punched in the police station's number, which I knew by heart, having called it so many times over the years.

It rang a long while, until Claire finally answered.

"Oh, hi, Jay."

"Claire, I need to talk to Turley. Where is he?"

"Um . . ." Pause. "He and Pat just walked outside with your brother."

"What are they doing outside?"

She sighed heavily, like you do right before delivering unwelcomed news. "I guess they want him down in Concord. I'm sorry, Jay. That detective came back up for him. Remember him? McGreevy?"

"Claire, you have to stop them. You hear me? Do not let him take Chris!"

"Um, I think you need to talk to Pat or Turley."

"There's no time! Please!"

"Oh, wait. Here he is, Jay."

The phone was set down on the other end, and I could hear the muffled chatter of joking voices in the background. It felt like an eternity before Turley finally picked up, though it had probably been only a few seconds.

"Oh, hey, Jay. Was about to call you. McGreevy is taking your brother down to Concord. But don't worry. He hasn't been charged with—"

"Listen to me, Turley. Listen to me carefully. You have to stop them. You hear me? Do not let McGreevy leave with my brother."

"Calm down, Jay."

"Do not let them leave! Stop them!"

"I can't do that, Jay."

"He's not a real cop."

"What?"

"McGreevy is dead. That guy isn't McGreevy!"

"Huh? Jay, you're not making any—"

"I'm on the way. I'll explain everything when I get there. Do not let them leave!"

"I can't do that," he said. "I mean, they . . . they're already gone."

"What! When?"

"Just now. When I walked inside."

"When, exactly?"

"Literally, less than a minute ago. But I'm telling you—"

I dropped the receiver and took off out the door, Charlie running after me. I hurdled down the front steps into the freshly settled night, a light snow beginning to fall, big soft balls floating like tufts of eiderdown. I patted my pockets for my truck keys.

"What are you gonna do?" Charlie asked.

I climbed into my Chevy. "Find them."

"I'll come with you."

"No. You stay here." I didn't know how this was going to play out, and I didn't want to involve Charlie any more than I already had. I jabbed the key in the ignition and fired my engine. "I'll call you."

"There's two ways out of town, Jay."

"They're going to Concord."

"How do you know?"

He was right. McGreevy was a Concord cop. Only this wasn't the real McGreevy. They'd catch the Turnpike, either south to Concord or north to Canada, it was a crapshoot, and I couldn't cover both on my own.

"I'll take the Turnpike north," Charlie said. "Just in case."

"Okay," I said. "Call me if you see them."

"Go! We've got to catch them before the turnoff to the Interstate. Once they hit the 93, we don't stand a chance."

I peeled out of Charlie's driveway, making for Camel's Back and Axel Rod Road. The country skies grew darker. I hooked a hard left, tires squealing as I swerved onto Orchard Drive, back end fishtailing all over the goddamn place.

I panned up and down the long street. If they were going south, they'd have to take Orchard. It was the most direct shot to the Turnpike. Nothing. Even if they were going north, they'd still have to access Orchard eventually. I couldn't have missed them. There weren't any streetlights in the cuts, but I should've at least been able to make out tail lights in the distance. I couldn't see a damn thing. They wouldn't be leisurely sightseeing through the center of town; they'd be on the move. They had to be around here somewhere. If you wanted out of Ashton, the Turnpike was your only option. Unless you took Christy Lane to Ragged Pass, and tried to go over the summit. But who would do that? After Lamentation Bridge and Echo Lake, there was nothing but dead-end cul-de-sacs and quaint neighborhoods in the foothills. And no one went farther than that. The peak itself was a deathtrap, especially in the winter. That high up, Lamentation Mountain's dirt roads carved through crags and gullies, meandering for miles, growing narrower and narrower, more hazardous by the minute. You could disappear in its shadows forever, and no one would even know you were missing . . .

I slammed on my brakes, flipped a bitch and made for Christy Lane, pushing seventy on the slick, icy street. I took the turn going so fast, my headlights barely provided any lead time to react to the hairpins and hazards. But this was my town; I could drive these roads blindfolded.

Ice and stone kicked up, dirtying high beams, hands shaking in a fit, though whether from the cold or chest-pounding anxiety, I couldn't be sure. I grabbed my cell to call Charlie. No bars. No surprise. I was on my own.

The moon tucked behind dense banks of storm clouds as I down-shifted my Chevy into second and began to climb the snaking, bumpy terrain toward the watershed. Coming upon Lamentation Bridge and Echo Lake, still not seeing their vehicle, I realized the foolish mistake I'd made following my gut on a whim. I pounded my steering wheel. Of course McGreevy, or whatever his name was, would make for the Turnpike. Get the fuck out of Dodge as fast as possible. I must've just missed them. They probably left earlier than Turley had said, which meant it was over. Even if I turned around now and hit one hundred, they'd have already made the Turnpike. Once there, they'd blend into the chaos of traffic and truckers, hit the Interstate and be long gone. I didn't even know what kind of vehicle they were driving. The only reason to come this way was if McGreevy's impersonator planned on killing my brother, sawing a hole in the ice, and sending him to a cold, watery grave, which seemed too surreal to grasp.

Besides my brother's potential murder, losing Chris now would mean no more time to right any ships, no more opportunities to reach an understanding. All the distance between my brother and me, never broached, all that water under the bridge, swept out to sea, with no chance for reconciliation. And just as I thought this, I caught the dim red glow of tail lights ascending Ragged Pass.

I punched the Chevy into gear, kicking cylinders into overdrive. Floored it, V-8 torqueing with a rush and a push; I took serious air over ramps of bedrock. Tires gaining traction, I gave that machine all she could handle, big block thrumming under the hood, 367 horsepower wailing. An ordinary car, in these conditions, didn't stand a chance. My headlights soon fanned the rear window. I could see Chris cuffed in the backseat.

The Pass had no guardrails. When people did venture up here, usually teenagers looking to party, it was during the daylight and warmer months when they could navigate slowly. We were in a high-speed car chase in the dead of night and the middle of winter.

My big truck could easily ram the fake McGreevy's puny car off the road, sending him careening down the mountainside. Except that my brother was in that car too.

I saw a flash of light first and then I heard the blast of gunshot. Both hands gripped firmly on the wheel, I ducked down and swerved, grinding gravel and gears, not surrendering an inch.

Having lived here my whole life, I knew about the turnaround coming up, less than a third of the way to the summit, a tortuous turn nicknamed Dead Man's Curve. I had less than half a mile, but if I could wedge around them, get out in front, I could broadside the Chevy and force them to stop. It wasn't the best plan. I didn't have a gun, which this guy clearly did, and I'd be putting myself right in the line of fire, in more ways than one. What choice did I have? I wasn't letting this sonofabitch take my brother. There was nothing stopping this guy from turning around at any minute and putting a bullet in Chris' brain. The second I gave him any relief, he'd realize that. I strapped on my seatbelt.

Fifty yards from the turnabout, I punched it hard, tires spinning on the steep incline, until my machine dug down deep, took root in the earth, and with a thunderous surge rocketed me past, wrenching loose both side-view mirrors in a shower of sparks. I slammed on the brakes, spinning 360° on the snow and ice, squared up in time to see a pair of headlights gunning straight for me. I braced for the collision. The impact was fast, fierce, furious, whipping me around and crumpling my driver's side door, snapping my head into the glass and leaving an instant spider web crack. But my truck was too big to get pushed around much, its sturdy steel frame and body absorbing the brunt of impact. The car that struck me—not so lucky. It sprung back into itself like a dejected Slinky, windshield exploding and splashing down diamonds, then stopped dead in its tracks. Smoke billowed from beneath its hood, and the car began slowly slipping on the ice, rotating around, gaining enough speed until the nose pointed downhill. It hopped the ledge where a guardrail should have been, balanced momentarily, like a teeter-totter on a parapet, before dropping twenty feet, headfirst into a boulder.

I unhooked my seatbelt. My door was jammed. I slid out the passenger side, rushing, limping, to the edge of the Pass. Down below, steam continued to stream from the engine, rear-end sticking straight in the air like a diver who'd misjudged the depth and dove straight into the mud.

I clasped onto frozen berry branches, using stumps for footholds, whatever could give me some traction to navigate the slippery, rocky, terrain.

"Chris!" I called out.

Nothing came back but country stillness.

Then I heard a faint cry.

Pressing forward, I slipped and fell on my ass, sliding a few feet and thwacking the back of my head before popping up, right beside the driver's side door, where, for all I knew, I could be greeted by a gun in my face.

Except, I wasn't. And the guy in the driver's seat wasn't going to be sticking a gun in anyone's face, ever again.

The fake McGreevy's head lay on the dash, blood trickling from the corner of his mouth, eyes locked in a death gaze. I checked for a pulse, just in case. He was already stiffening up. I could see my brother stirring in the back. I rifled through the dead man's pockets, searching until I found his wallet. I flipped it open. There was the badge. And right beside it a driver's license. Roger Paul, New York City. Ashton's finest had handed my brother off to this guy to be killed.

"Chris! Chris?"

My brother groaned.

"Hold on," I said, "I'm getting you out of here."

I felt in the hitman's jacket and retrieved the keys for the handcuffs. Then I saw the 9mm on the seat beside him. The last time I'd fired a gun was at beer cans up at Coal Creek. I stuck the pistol in the back of my pants.

I moved to the rear, opening the door. "Can you move? Anything broken?"

Chris flopped around, arms still cuffed behind him, pencil-thin neck cocked at an odd angle. Between the straggled strands of bleached blond hair, he had a giant gash on his forehead, and that goofy grin on his face.

"Hey, little brother," he said wearily, pushing through a smile. "I knew you wouldn't let me down."

CHAPTER TWENTY-ONE

I couldn't think of anywhere else to go. My apartment was obviously out. So too Charlie's. We were already on the mountain and not far from the foothills. Thank God the truck still turned over when I tried starting it.

The only person who knew about Ben Saunders' place was my boss, Tom, and he was out of town for the next couple weeks. Sure, they'd eventually reach out to him, probably sooner than later, but it bought us some time. And I had the 9mm. I was convincing myself by the minute I'd use it if I had to. I wasn't thinking so great, honestly. In the thin mountain air, oxygen doesn't flow to your brain, synapses misfire, connections don't get made. Smacking your skull against glass in a high-speed car crash doesn't help, either. It's not the best time to be trying to solve math equations. All I knew was that, until I figured this mess out, we were holing up at the old farmhouse.

I steered the battered Chevy up the driveway. The U-Haul had been removed, carted off by Tom. I killed the lights, opened the garage, and gazed over the barren countryside. No neighbors for miles, the homestead ghostly. The snow came down steadily now and was starting to accumulate at my feet.

I latched the overhead doors and sealed us in, then helped my brother out of the truck. He winced as I let him lean the full weight of his body on me. The burden wasn't great. He felt as wasted away as a cancer patient in the late stages. I let us into the vestibule with the key I'd never given back to Tom.

The only creature comforts that remained: a folding patio chair and a fire-damaged carpet in the living room. I'd thrown my jacket over

Chris' bum overcoat at the accident site, but he still shivered violently; it was every bit as cold inside the house as it was out. With the hit to his head and a bleeding gash, I worried he'd go into shock. I sat him by the fireplace while I went scouring for blankets or towels, old sheets, anything Tom might've left behind to help keep us from freezing to death. All I found was the stack of newspapers I'd been using to wrap valuables.

Then I remembered the cord of wood I'd tripped over in the pantry, when I cut myself on that exposed nail. Hard to believe it had been only four days ago.

I considered the smoke coming from the chimney, but quickly dismissed any concern. The only way someone might see the smoke through this storm was if they were coming here anyway. And if they were coming here anyway, what difference did it make? It wasn't a tough call. I could hear Chris' teeth chattering all the way in the kitchen. What was left of them, at least.

Stacking the wood in a pyramid, I crinkled the old, dry newspaper, stuffing wadded sheets evenly, making sure they were perfectly spaced out, and got a flashback of my father doing the same. Down on a knee, arms thick as railroad ties, sweat stains pooled under pits, focused intently on the task at hand. Funny, when I pictured my father, didn't matter the memory, he was never looking at me. Anytime I thought of him, he was watching someone else, doing something else, engaged in a random chore, but never meeting my eyes. Flames licked the parched newsprint, sparking the wood, and soon a fire raged.

Chair and all, I dragged my brother as close to the heat as I could without burning him. He was nearly convulsive, he was so cold. I wrapped my arms tightly around him, rubbing his back, trying to warm him. I knelt down and checked the wound on his head. I couldn't see much, the cut smeared and crusted over, mingling with the layers of homeless dirt.

I went to the kitchen. Water still worked. Wet my shirttail, then cleaned Chris' cut. The bleeding had stopped. When I washed away the dried blood, I saw the gash wasn't as deep as I'd originally feared. In fact, once cleaned off, it wasn't much more than a scratch.

"It's getting dark, Doc," Chris rasped, shaking with exaggerated palsy. "Smoke? Can I get a last smoke?" He laughed. And instantly stopped the phony seizures. This was my brother's fucked-up sense of humor, mocking my motherly concern.

"Sure. Laugh it up." I plopped on my ass and watched the flames dance, bathing the musty old room in a brilliant amber-orange hue. Shadows stretched across the hardwood, up water-stained walls, rendering my brother and me distorted versions of ourselves.

I tossed him the cigarette pack. He bent far forward and lit one directly from the fire.

"How'd you know that guy wasn't really a cop?" he asked me, hopping up, suddenly spry.

"Fisher. You remember him?"

"Sure. You went to second base with his girlfriend back in high school. Gina something. Said she had a terrific rack."

"How the fuck do you remember that?"

"Because you told me."

Guy couldn't get it together long enough to visit a dentist, but he remembered me copping a feel in the tenth grade.

"Whatever. So Fisher works as an investigator for an insurance company down in Concord, and he recognized the name. Seems a couple weeks ago, this detective turns up dead. Anyways, doesn't matter now. The important part is, we figured it out as they were handing you over."

"You tell Turley?"

"I tried to. Wasn't a lot of time. Anyone pretending to be a cop wasn't taking you for ice cream." I looked up at him from the floor. "When did you figure it out?"

He screwed up his face like he had to think about it. "Probably when he said he was going to shoot me in the head and bury me beneath the ice."

"You could've told him I had the disc."

"For what? So he could cut a hole big enough for two?" Chris turned. "Did you look at it?"

"Yeah. So did Fisher and Charlie."

"And?"

"And . . . I can't say for sure. Could be Mr. Lombardi. There's not much to go on. Only a couple pics show a face. Grainy as hell." I reached to get back my cigarettes.

"That's what I figured. Pretty stupid of me, eh?"

"I don't know, Chris. Guy has the same hunched posture, and the computer *did* come from Lombardi. If you'd gotten more evidence, maybe you could've—"

"What? Been a hero?" He winced a grin.

"Did that Roger Paul guy say who he worked for?"

"Didn't have to," Chris said, drawing deeply on his cigarette. "So what's the plan, Wyatt Earp? We gonna smoke 'em outta their holes?" He laughed until he coughed a fit.

Despite his "What, me worry?" act, my brother looked more peaked, drained, emaciated than usual. I was hardly an expert on the drug lifestyle and its physical toll, but I knew once you'd been on them long enough, you started needing them to survive, like food. And, boy, did he look hungry.

"Haven't really thought this through, little brother, have you?"

"Didn't exactly have the option of planning." I checked my phone. Again. No bars. No surprise.

"You know they can trace your cell? Tri-ang-u-late," he said, pronouncing every syllable. "They're gonna find us eventually, you know that, right?"

I tried to formulate an escape, conceive a plan. Nothing doing. I felt hopeless.

"It was an accident," Chris said. "Guy wasn't even a real cop. Maybe they'll just give you a stern warning this time. Get off with community service. I'm not sure vehicular manslaughter is even a crime anymore." He chuckled.

"There's nothing funny about any of this."

Chris arched his back, stretching until he yawned. "Good call on the fire." He peeled off my jacket and tossed it to me, shaking off his overcoat, quaking till he busted out a jellied shimmy. "You should just drive back."

"And what about you?"

"What about me?" He smiled. "Don't you know it's too late for me, little brother?"

"You don't have to keep living this way," I said. "You could get your ass straightened out, get a regular place to live, a job. You're not even forty yet."

My brother wrinkled his mouth. "I've been at it too long."

"Bullshit. You could quit if you wanted to."

"You're right," he said. "And I don't want to."

"How the hell can you say that? You want your teeth falling out? You want to sleep outside in the freezing cold? Sell your body? For what? Are the drugs really that good?"

"The truth? I don't even feel them anymore." My brother reached for the sky, threadbare T-shirt rising. I could count each bony rib in the firelight. "I only feel it when I don't do them." He winked, then walked to the window. "No, I'm in too deep this time, and I don't have the energy to fight my way out."

"What did you really do?" I said. "You broke into a house, a job site, so what?" I didn't add that he'd also beaten the shit out of a man and broken his arm, trusting Turley at his word that he'd be able to keep that one off the books.

"I don't have an alibi for the night Pete died."

"But you didn't do it."

He didn't respond.

I waited.

"Right?"

Slowly, he shook his head no. "People heard me making threats, though. I was his friend, his partner. I don't have an alibi. And Adam and Michael know I know, and they won't take a chance I'll talk. I don't have any leverage."

"We have that disc, right?"

"No one can prove that's Gerry Lombardi in those pictures. You said so yourself."

"We could at least turn it over to the cops. The accusation alone—"

"From a junkie like me?"

"I'll back you up."

"Now why the hell would you do something like that?"

"I have a son of my own. I can't let a monster like that run loose. It's sick. It's wrong."

"You're not even certain it's Gerry Lombardi."

"But you are."

"Yes. I am."

"Then that's good enough for me. I'll back you up. We take the disc, go to the cops. The press. Full-on assault."

"You want to take on Adam and Michael Lombardi? Then you'll have them after you too. No, little brother, I can't let you do that. You're right. You have a son. And you need to be there for him. This is a losing battle, and only one captain needs to go down with this ship." He started humming, then singing quietly, swaying gently in waltz timing. I couldn't make out the tune until I heard the words "Gitche Gumee," and then I recognized "The Wreck of the Edmund Fitzgerald."

"Will you knock it off?"

"Does anyone know where the love of God goes?" he sang, earnestly. "When the waves turn the minutes to hours?"

"Is everything a joke to you?" I said. "I know it wasn't easy for you when they died. And I know it got you started on whatever this . . . this thing is you're on. But regardless of what you think, it's not too late. It's *never* too late. We can check you in somewhere, get you help. I mean it. I'll vouch for you with this disc, back you up all the way."

"You're not really dumb enough to stick your neck out for me, are you?" He sighed. "When will you stop being such a hard case? I saw the way Jenny was looking at you. When I said you still loved her, she blushed, right in the middle of that shit storm. She blushed." Chris flicked his butt into the fire. "What are you waiting for? You're wasting your life."

"I'm wasting my life? Oh, that's rich. This coming from the guy who hangs out at truck stops . . ." I caught myself. "You don't understand. I'm not husband material. I'm not father material. I'm not cut out for it like Dad was. I can't do that domestic shit. I can't give Jenny and Aiden what they need. They're better off—"

"What? With an abusive asshole like Brody? Give me a break. You're acting like a chickenshit coward, and you're selling yourself short. You think you can't measure up to our father, so you don't bother trying."

He turned slightly over his shoulder. The flames carved up his cadaverous features.

This might've been the most honest conversation I'd ever had with my brother. And I hated him for doing this to me now.

"What would you know about it, Chris? You take nothing seriously. You take no responsibility for anything."

"I did it," my brother said, as casually as if he were confessing to eating the last cupcake, or leaving behind an empty container of milk in the fridge.

"Did what?" I asked, agitated.

"What they say I did."

My only thought was Pete, which made no sense, since we'd just talked about that. "You're changing your story now? Telling me you murdered Pete? I don't believe you. You're being ridiculous. Five minutes ago—"

"Not Pete," he said.

A chill ran through me.

He turned back around, talking through the glass, as if to the night. I watched his breath spread over the windowpane, cracking silver ice on a mountain lake.

"I waited for the night of the Merriman's annual Christmas party," he said, "because I knew he'd take Lamentation Bridge. The bridge always ices over that time of year."

"What are you—"

"I'd driven with him enough to know he took Lamentation Bridge faster than he should, especially when he'd had a couple drinks, and he *always* had a couple drinks before the Merriman's party. Of course, I couldn't have known it would actually work. Brake lines snapping ain't an exact science." At this he peered over his shoulder at me, a wicked glint in his eye. "But it didn't matter, Jay. If it hadn't worked that time, I'd have kept trying until it did."

"You're lying. Why are you saying this? You're lying."

He went back to talking softly to the night. "She knew," he said, voice so lulled it was almost a whisper. "The whole time, she knew. I wasn't going to let him do to you what he'd done to me." My brother let his head fall, resting on the cold glass.

I lowered my shoulder and tackled him to the ground. We crashed in a heap. The 9mm in the back of my pants fell out and slid across the floor. I had him pinned.

"That didn't happen!" I screamed into his face. I began raining blows on his chest. He didn't squirm or try to fight back. "You're making that up! Like that bullshit drowning story. And all your other bullshit stories." I grabbed him by the collar, shaking him violently. He responded like a limp rag doll, flopping about, googly eyes rolling back in his skull. "I know you're lying! Tell me you're lying!"

I let him go. His head thudded. He looked off to the side, like he'd grown disinterested in the conversation, sleepy, or simply bored.

"Was it Lombardi? Did he do that to you? Is that why you hate him? Is that what this is all about? Answer me, Chris!" I was almost crying. "Dad never did that. Tell me you're lying. Tell me that never happened."

"I've told so many stories," my brother said. "I'm not sure what's even true anymore."

We both fell silent.

Feedback hissed from a bullhorn. Flashing colors swirled through the windows like a kaleidoscope. White-hot spotlight poured in.

"Come out with your hands on your head!"

That wasn't Pat or Turley.

I dragged Chris away from the window, sticking him in the corner away from an open shot. I picked up the 9mm from the floor and pointed it at him. "Stay there!"

This wasn't happening.

I peeked out the kitchen window. There were a lot of cop cars, way more than Ashton's limited fleet. And more were speeding up the driveway, sirens sounding, blues and reds whirling, tires screeching to a halt.

I crept toward the front door. I heard Chris walk into the kitchen behind me.

"They want me, Jay. Not you."

"Shut up. Let me think. I told you not to move!"

"Lombardi won't stop."

I spun around. "That isn't Adam or Michael Lombardi out there. Those are cops."

"Those aren't Ashton cops. They're not putting me in the county jail this time. I'm going to prison, little brother. I'll be dead before breakfast. There's no way I walk out of here alive."

"Stay put and let me handle this."

"Jay, it's me, Turley. I need you and your brother to come out. Hands on your head. Okay? We've got to straighten this out, Jay. It's not too late to straighten this all out. Come out with your hands up."

"He wasn't a cop!" I shouted back.

"I know. Now come out with your hands on your head before someone else gets hurt!"

There was a seismic shrill as the megaphone was ripped from Turley's grip.

The police switched off their lights, casting the house in total darkness.

"This is Lester Gibbons of the Concord Police. Exit the premises now with your hands on your head. This is the last time you will be instructed to do so. You have thirty seconds to comply."

"Or what?" I shouted back.

"What are you planning on doing, little brother? Going out like Butch and Sundance?" Chris chuckled in the dark.

Beyond the door, I could hear muffled orders given, the scatter of feet getting in position, weapons cocked and mounted, ready to fire on a single command.

All I wanted in that moment was to be back with Jenny and my son. My family. Just the three of us, in a cozy house, somewhere far from here. I swore to God and the heavens above that if He could just get me out of this mess, I'd make it right. No matter what. I'd make it right.

Then there was a loud crack, like glass shattering, a flashbang exploding in a brilliant wave of light, and I felt all my weight being pulled down.

I crashed to the dusty floor as Chris blew past me out the front door.

Gunfire erupted all around.

And then I was out.

CHAPTER TWENTY-TWO

Turned out my brother had no trouble knocking me unconscious in the dark, after all.

He'd probably hit me harder than he'd intended. Or maybe not. Between brothers, there's always sibling rivalry. This was his free pass. To haul off and slug me and still come off looking like the good guy. I went down hard. Maybe it was more than getting blindsided by a patio chair. Maybe I'd collapsed from the weight of it all. Either way, I came to in the hospital. The doctors said I had a mild concussion.

I knew what had happened before anyone told me. I could've dreamt it, or perhaps I'd overheard someone talking in my sleep.

What did it matter now? My brother was gone.

After he'd slugged me, Chris had taken the 9mm from me when I fell, stepped outside, and waved it around like a lunatic. Suicide by cop, they called it.

That's how everything got wrapped up. No Butch and Sundance. No grand finale. Just a junkie checking out because he was too tired to go on, which left me with more questions than I'd ever get answers to. What else was new? When it came to my brother, you had to divide by four to get at the truth. Charges of molestation. Saving kids from drowning. Cutting brake lines. Lombardi. My father. Who did what to whom. Who knows? Chris was right about one thing, though. I don't think even he knew what was real anymore.

The rest was easier to ascertain. When I took off after Chris, Fisher had picked up the phone and filled in Turley, who immediately called Concord PD, only to get confirmation that the man calling himself

McGreevy wasn't actually McGreevy. The revelation that someone had been impersonating a dead Concord detective had unleashed a wave of real Concord cops onto the scene. Which was a bit of irony, if you think about it.

Roger Paul, it would be determined, had been collecting on a drug debt. A ridiculous and flimsy cover, but probably the most convenient way to sweep an embarrassing problem under the rug. Which worked in my favor too, since there are no vehicular manslaughter charges for scumbag-on-scumbag crime. Perhaps Turley and Pat parlayed whatever favor they had for my benefit. Or, more likely, no one gave a shit about two dead lowlifes. Certainly, no one had tied Roger Paul to the Lombardis, and I didn't offer any theories. I made sure Fisher and Charlie didn't, either.

I don't know what would've happened if Chris had given himself up, whether he might've been able to explain he didn't kill Pete, or, with everything out in the open, if Adam or Michael or whoever would've had no choice but to back off and let events take their natural course. But in the weeks following my release from the hospital, as everything returned to normal, or as normal as things would ever be, I saw that my brother had been right not to bother trying. The riptide that took hold of his life had dragged him out to a rough sea too damn deep and dirty to wade out of clean. When you hit the point of no return, I guess you keep going and see what's on the other side. I hated him for not giving me the chance to say goodbye, but in moments like that, I guess nobody gets a happy send-off.

* * *

The funeral took place on a cold, brisk February day. Most of the town came to pay their respects. People from Chris' graduating class and from the wrestling team, guys he hadn't talked to in years; Turley, and Pat, who'd officially announced his retirement; Claire Sizemore, Fisher, and, of course, Jenny and Aiden. I even saw Adam Lombardi lurking in the back row when I got up to deliver my eulogy at the church, dressed sharply, there to represent the entire Lombardi family. I wasn't surprised to see him. He'd never miss the opportunity for face time or, more accurately, risk being perceived negatively, especially not with his new ski resort about to break ground. He'd come without his bodyguard. Maybe Erik Bowman and his Commanderoes buddies no longer ran security for him. Or, maybe the situation didn't require their presence. For such a small town, it was a helluva turnout.

At the wake afterwards, which we held at Charlie's, since he had the nicest house, I tried not to get too bogged down by a somber mood. In those situations, everyone is coming up to you saying the same thing, how sorry they are for your loss, urging you to remember the good times, and those are nice things to say, and they are nice things to hear. But, not really. They're things you have to say, like when someone's mother has cancer and you ask if there's anything you can do, knowing damn well there's not.

We had a big spread, generously paid for by Tom Gable, who joked that it was my severance package, since I'd told him I couldn't work for him anymore, now that I'd be moving to Concord. Fisher had helped me land a job with his company down there. I'd be starting on the ground floor. But I didn't mind having to work my way up. For some reason, I felt hungrier than I had in a long time.

After I'd shaken enough hands and thanked enough people for coming, I told Jenny I'd be outside. She gave me a sweet kiss, and I put my arms around her. Nobody had seen Brody since he cleared out his shit and headed off for Rutland, alone. He must've known he lost more in that kitchen than just a fight with my junkie brother. Jenny and Aiden had picked me up from the hospital and taken me home. They never left. We'd spent practically every waking second together since. Nothing had ever felt more right.

Standing on Charlie's porch, smoking a cigarette, I stared at Lamentation Mountain, a cool breeze washing over me. I felt a hand on my shoulder, and turned to see Adam Lombardi. I'd been expecting him, sooner or later. He left his hand there for a while, staring with me, like the view meant something to him too.

"I'm sorry for your loss," he said. "I know it ended badly. But your brother and I were friends once."

"A long time ago."

He chuckled politely, always the politician.

"Saw in the paper they won't be renewing the lease for the truck stop. Guess that frees up the land for your big ski resort."

"It's more complicated than that," Adam said, his tone downshifting to condescending. "But, yes, plans are moving forward to build a resort there. Going to be quite a boon for this town."

I dragged on my cigarette. "Especially for you and your brother."

"It's going to be good for everyone, Jay." He squeezed my shoulder and descended the stairs.

"For your dad too, I'm sure."

He stopped and turned around.

"Gerry's getting old," I said. "I think he needs to take what little time he has left to enjoy the spoils."

Adam grinned tersely. "I'll be sure to tell him you said hello."

"I'm thinking more like, it might be time for him to retire. Stop participating in UpStart, give up coaching wrestling too. I mean, what I'm trying to say, Adam, is that your dad needs to spend more time at home."

Adam took a step back toward me, eyes whittled. "It's nice of you to be so concerned, Jay. But that's not your decision to make."

"I think it is." I dropped my cigarette and squashed it with my heel, stepping to him and standing toe to toe. "You know, before my brother died, he showed me some interesting—I guess interesting isn't the right word, more like, fucking disturbing—pictures."

Adam glanced off, feigning indifference, before turning back extra bemused. "Why would I care?"

"I guess you wouldn't. But other people might." I grinned. "I made a few copies of a disc with those pictures. Have them sitting in a few places. All over Ashton. Instructions to open at a later date, under certain circumstances, y'know, if something should happen to me and all that."

"Whatever you're trying to say, Jay, just say it. Don't get cute. I don't have time."

"Okay," I said. "I'm moving down to Concord with my fiancée and son, and if I don't hear within the week that your father has quit coaching, and stepped down from the UpStart board, I'm going to send that disc to every newspaper and television station in New Hampshire."

Adam smirked.

I waved my hand. "You go build your ski resort. Help your brother get reelected to another term. Make a lot of money. But if your sick fuck of a pedophile father isn't under self-imposed house arrest, I'll release those pictures, I swear to God I will. And maybe it won't be enough to get him to spend the rest of his life in prison where he belongs, but it certainly will be enough to scare off potential investors and derail political aspirations. Innuendo and rumor go a long way in a small town."

I heard the screen door open and shut behind me. Charlie and Jenny, who held my sleepy son, came to stand beside me.

"Thanks for coming, Adam," I said. "Your kind words mean a lot."

He forced a smile and said goodbye.

Skulking across the driveway, Adam Lombardi climbed in his Land Rover and roared off.

Other folks began leaving as well, the party breaking up.

"I've got to get Aiden down for his nap," Jenny said. "You all right?"

"Never been better."

She leaned over and kissed me. "See you at home?"

"It's only our home for another week," I said. "Then I'm getting us a new one."

Jenny smiled, cradling Aiden's sleepy head, which I kissed gently.

Charlie and I walked around the side of his house. He pulled two beers from inside his coat, passing one over. We clinked bottles.

"What'd Lombardi have to say?"

"Not much."

"You tell him about the discs?"

"Yup."

"Think he bought it?"

"I don't know." I shrugged. "Worth a shot, right?"

"Guess we'll never know for sure if that was Gerry Lombardi in those pictures, eh?"

I shrugged again like I agreed, and fired another cigarette. But I already had my answer.

We stayed like that for a moment, silently staring over the horizon as the low winter sun set behind Lamentation.

"Saw you talking to Tom Gable," I said.

Charlie flashed a devil's grin. "As luck would have it, he's looking for help."

"You sure about this? No benefits. No union."

"No waking up every morning with a hole in my belly, feeling like I want to die. I'll take my chances. Besides, if it doesn't work out, it doesn't work out. I'll find something else. Life's too short to be spending every day doing something you hate."

"You're still helping me move next weekend?"

"You bet."

"You're going to get down and visit once in a while, right?"

"Of course. But you'll be back plenty. You've lived in Concord before. You always come back. Fisher always comes back. Everyone comes back. Ashton is like herpes. Can't escape it."

I drained a slug of beer, and handed Charlie the half-full bottle. "You need me to help clean up?"

"Nah," Charlie said. "Get home to your wife and son."

"She's not my wife yet."

"She will be soon enough," he replied with a grin. "Face it, Jay. Ain't no running from it anymore. You're a family man now."

I had to admit. I liked the sound of that.

CPSIA information can be obtained
at www.ICGtesting.com
Printed in the USA
FSHW011114140121
77609FS

9 781608 091850